Passenger

(A Divinely Inspired Comedy in 13 Books)

By: Tygarjas Twyrls Bigstyck

"Passenger: A Divinely Inspired Comedy in 13 Books," by Tygarjas Twyrls Bigstyck. ISBN 978-1-60264-577-6 (softcover); 978-1-60264-633-9 (hardcover).

Library of Congress Control Number: 2010928583.

Published 2010 by Virtualbookworm.com Publishing Inc., P.O. Box 9949, College Station, TX 77842, US.

Manufactured in the United States of America.

Commentary by the author:

You may take it as a metaphor, you may take it at face value. You may take it for its symbolism, or stagnating lack thereof. You may take it as fact, or you may take it as fiction. You may take it as a simple story, no more, no less, or you may spend your life analyzing it to death. You may take it as you like, or you may leave it if you dare. But, when all is said and done, it is only what it is, and you will see it as you are.

For all those in my life whom I have called "Teacher,"

For **_She_**, who returned to me _my_ breath.

For my Father-Mother who art in Heaven, _and_ one Earth,
Haloed be _Our_ name.

Do you remember?
Hearts were too cold
Seasons had frozen us
Into our souls

People were saying
The whole world is burning
Ashes were scattered
Too hard to turn

Upside out
Or inside down
False alarm, the only game in town
No man's land, the only game in town
Terrible, the only game in town

Passenger
-Peter Monk

                              Believe it implicitly
                               Love is tranquility
                             If you don't know that
                             Then nothing is known

                                  Lady Simplicity
                                  -Robert Hunter

Speak muse of *One*
on a journey without end.
Knowing all of Life's joys,
and, knowing all of Life's sufferings.
Knowing Heaven,
and, Knowing Hell.
Knowing Death,
and, Knowing Life.

Book 1
The Bus Arrives On Time or *All* Aboard!

He caught the last bus leaving after he had finished work at the data processing office. He walked up the stairs of the bus; the door of the bus shut quickly behind him with a definitive "CLACK!" and the wheels of the bus began to roll 'round. The bus was empty save for the seats, the driver and himself. He heard a voice that sent a sudden chill down his spine, and the words formed by that voice, "Destination Hell, please take your seat!"

Looking up quickly to the driver's face, Tim gasped in horror to see a sight he could not believe. Matching the voice he couldn't believe he had heard was the face which was impossible for him to be seeing, that of his father. Gawking for a moment in disbelief, Tim hesitantly forced himself to speak, "A . . . Are you my father? I mean, you look just like . . . and . . . and you sound exactly— . . . But, you died . . . I mean . . . the casket . . . it was closed . . . and I couldn't bring myself to . . . I mean, that's not how I wanted to remember . . . But Mom, she saw and . . . the news . . . the bus *did* crash . . . and you . . . what . . . what is this? Who are you?"

A grim chuckle and a minor laugh arose from the driver's lips. Full lips, amazingly smooth and attached to a face that looked about 50 years of age with a moderately long, full, snow-white beard. "Son," the man began, "as I stated a very short while ago, you have just boarded a bus with Hell as its destination. Don't fret, there'll be a couple of stops along the way where you can stretch your legs, but you won't be leaving this ride until we have reached the bus's destination, the very heart of Hell. Now, if you would be so kind as to take a seat, I believe you will find that once you settle yourself into a comfortable sitting position, you will have a much smoother and more pleasant ride. Oh, and to answer your other question, your father was a good man who knew the light of the gate of Heaven and will reside in said realm for an indefinite period, and has hope of transcending even that place. But, I find I am weaving from the straightest path that answers your question, so, to put it into simple terms that you may begin to be able to grasp, let's just say that my form and voice are presented to you as they are to make your journey a bit more . . .palatable."

Tim wanted off, but in the short time he had mumbled his disbelief and the driver had responded, already the bus had passed the onramp and begun speeding north on Highway 101. Even if Tim could get away with opening or breaking a window or a door, a leap out of a bus at this speed would be suicide, and that's if there happened to be no cars to hit him when he hit the ground.

Tim took a seat as the driver had bid him do and sat quietly in a deep confusion for several minutes, trying to make sense out of his situation and reconcile the fact that this was no dream. And, assuming that this really was happening, what had he done to warrant . . . Hell? He didn't attend church every single week perhaps, but he tried to live up to his faith. He tried to do the right thing. Maybe he had had sex out of wedlock and liked to drink a beer every now and then, but he was neither a womanizer nor an alcoholic by any stretch of the imagination. He wasn't a thief. He tried to remain humble and true to his belief in one God. He hadn't killed anyone. Maybe a fistfight or two under extreme circumstances, but neither party died and the other guy never looked worse than he did when all was said and done. God knew as well as he that he wasn't perfect, but Hell? Was he really *Hell* worthy?

The bus was now passing San Francisco International airport, and the bus seemed to be going toward the city. Normally Tim would have been very happy to be heading into San Francisco, he loved the city. He loved the music and the theatre. He loved being able to get the best Chinese food in the country in the first Chinatown in North America. He loved the wharf and the bustle and the hipsters who still made the city what it was 40 years after the days of the flower children and the hippies. He didn't always care for the level of crime or various unpleasant characters that one might sometimes run into in entire sections of the city, but as a whole, he loved the life that ran through the city and usually loved spending any time there he could. Today, however, as much as he may have wanted to be overjoyed to be heading into the city, he simply couldn't pull his attention away from the fact that his ride was taking place on a bus that his dead father was driving, apparently to bring him to Hell.

After processing his thoughts for the better part of twenty minutes, Tim finally felt as though he should try to attempt speech again. He began to form a question with the best of his ability considering his circumstances. "Am I dead? I mean, how . . . when . . . how did I . . . die? Why Hell? I went to chur— . . . I never . . . no murder . . . no cheating . . . stealing. What did I . . . why Hell?"

"You know, boy," began the driver, "my answers to your questions will be much easier for you to even *begin* to comprehend if you learn to ask just one at a time. But, to answer your previous string of questions, not to mention statements, I'll begin by telling you that you died just like your father in a horribly painful bus explosion on your way home from work. Talk about a coincidence, eh? Anyway, we have this 'sins of the fathers' clause that you had to fulfill, and basically since you had no son, the buck stopped with you, so to speak. Hit you doubly hard, in fact, because of the whole 'exact same death as Dad' thing. When all's said and done, all this combined earns you a one-way ticket to Hell."

Tim became deathly pale and extremely silent.

The driver turned his head to look at Tim, and then burst out in uncontrollable laughter. "A joke, a joke," chuckled the driver with a fat grin on his face. "Sorry 'bout that kid, I was just pullin' at ya a bit there. Look, from where I'm sittin', after an eternity and a half or so of carting folks to Hell as the general order of things, one's sense of humor can begin to warp a bit, if you catch my drift. I meant no ill by it. The truth is, slugger, I'm not really given the particulars of why a soul was separated from its body or what that soul did to earn itself a trip to ye olde place'o'damnation. Hey, if it's any consolation to you, that which arranges trips such as these does try to make the journey as smooth as possible. So, lay back, enjoy the view, and don't sweat it so much. There's nothing you can really do to change it anyway. It's a nice, long ride to Hell, so enjoy a last glimpse at this beautiful earthly plane you've called home for as long as you have, and I'm sure by the time it's time to get off the bus for good, all of your questions will have been answered."

Tim began again, "But why—"

"Look kiddo," the driver cut him off. "Heck! I probably can't answer whatever question you're going to ask anyway. Look, the why of just about any matter you could find to inquire after really isn't all that important. Like I was saying just a moment ago, the really important stuff lies a lot more in how you handle what you've got to work with. A big slab of rock in Michelangelo's hands, and you got a "David" that people rave about for God only knows why and for far longer than Michelangelo could have guessed. So, relax. Let yourself enjoy the ride. You'll be doing yourself a lot better than if you fret over the inevitable, eh?"

Tim was silent. He sat back watching the scenery roll by, and suddenly the world outside seemed a whole lot brighter. It was as though this road he had passed on many times, he had never noticed in such detail before. It was like living life with fresh eyes, newly grown with the knowledge that he was not likely to see any of what passed by his window ever again.

After another twenty minutes or so, the bus was still riding the 101 and, unless the road suddenly arose into the sky--or for that matter, lowered into the earth--the bus would be passing through the city shortly.

Sure enough, no roads approached lowering into Hell, and indeed, the skyline of the city did appear. Tim had assumed that the bus would be making for the shortest route to one of the city's two more famous bridges. He was surprised, therefore, when the bus turned onto an offramp and headed into the city's heart.

Tim began to lose his sense of complete terror and awe as they entered the thick of the city. There was something about the point of the Transamerica building, the smell of the bay, and Oriental characters on the windows of every other restaurant that had a naturally calming effect on Tim. Despite still having quite the appreciation for the world around him, and a subtle sense of horror running through his blood, in his head an obvious though improbable notion began with speed to form: ESCAPE!

He wasn't fully aware of this thought simmering in the back of his mind, a thought simmering since practically the second he had stepped onto the bus, until he saw the people of the city walking past the bus while it was stopped at a crosswalk. Perhaps the incredible improbability of getting out alive when on the highway had conditioned his mind against any sort of escape attempt, but now that the bus was frequently stopping completely in short intervals, and people were all around. Tim, for the first time since the ride began, took to the notion of fleeing a predicament he deemed worthy of dissociating himself from as quickly as humanly possible.

Thinking no time better to act toward getting the hell away from this hell bus destined for Hell, as the bus stopped at the next red light, one in which many pedestrians were passing in front of the bus, Tim flung himself at the bus's door with all his might, trying to get it open. Failing that, Tim tried to gain the attention of the passers by by flailing his limbs wildly, mixed with yelling and beating at the door with every ounce of strength he possessed. Tim pounded and pounded and grew noticeably red in the face as he used every bit of energy he could find in his being toward the end of trying to escape his unpleasant fate. He clawed at the windows, trying to find some way to break them or open them. He threw himself as hard as he could against windows and door alike.

The light turned green, the bus rolled on, and the driver spoke. "You know, had you beat just a teensy bit harder . . . still absolutely *nothing* would have happened. I bet you'd sell your soul to get away right about now, eh? Sorry kid, just a little satanic humor for you there. Look, kiddo, that which made this bus knew what they were doing when they put the thing together. And besides, as far as the earthly realm is concerned, you don't exist in the physical right now. Look, I'm not really supposed to be telling you this sort of thing 'til we exit "Earth proper," but for now, think of yourself as being on a non-interactive tour as a sort of final allowance, or "gift" if you will, of seeing a place you won't be seeing again for a good long while. Like say an eternity or two. Enjoy seeing of the Earth what you can *while* you can. As I've tried to tell you before, enjoy yourself while enjoyment is still an option."

Tim sat down again with the strong feeling that he had probably been better off when the notion of escape hadn't arisen to the top of his mind. If anything at all of benefit had come from his attempt to get away from this bus of ill omen, it was that he was now so utterly exhausted from exerting energy that for the first time since he had gotten on the bus, he began to give in to the urge to give up and let the bus take him wherever it intended on taking him. He was almost beginning to be able to relax, and that didn't feel altogether unpleasant, even though just about everything else regarding his situation did. So, Tim let his head rest against the window and watched the activity of the city as the bus rolled along.

Half an hour or so had passed when Tim noticed that the bus seemed to be heading toward the Castro district. Now, generally Tim was very accepting of people's varying perspectives, but there was definitely a feeling of discomfort that sparked within him at the sight of a pair of men holding hands. He may not have attended church every single week, and he may not even have taken just any old thing he had been taught to heart, but it seemed to him that there was absolutely a fundamental aberration to the order of nature that any pair of men would . . . choose to hold hands. It made sense to Tim that his priest, without absolutely damning homosexuality, did take a strong stance that homosexuality was not beneficial to what God had intended. He also felt that any doubt he might have about the validity of a blind belief, no matter how much sense it made, was absolutely affirmed by science. He could see easily the way of nature. Men were meant to be with women; otherwise both parties would have been designed differently. Homosexuality was so obviously a perversion of nature, and worse than that, he felt more often than not it must also be as much a distortion of the nature of the mind as of the body.

Suffice to say that while seeing two men hold hands caused Tim a spark of discomfort, at seeing more interaction than a simple grope of two hands Tim's spark would be fanned into something of a minor flame. Generally Tim would extricate himself from such awkward situations he might find himself in, lest his small flame of burning discomfort be fueled further. The one time he could recall being forced to drive through the Castro, he had endured a discomfort verging on what some might call a total psychotic meltdown. So, upon realizing, beyond any remaining shred of doubt or hope, that he was about to enter the Castro, a place historically less than comfortable for Tim, whatever shred of relaxation he had managed to grasp at since his failed attempt at escape was quickly replaced by a tension he did not think his body was physically capable of. He felt almost as though there were muscles tensing upon muscles which he hadn't thought existed within his body to begin with.

The bus entered that district so disquieting to Tim, and as it did, Tim's ease slipped swiftly from his being. The driver also seemed to tense a bit, though apparently not out of discomfort, but rather as though he was becoming more alert to the world around him.

At the outskirts of the district Tim would occasionally see a pair of women holding hands, which oddly enough he didn't seem to find much discomfort with at all, or a pair of men holding hands, which he felt discomfort at, but was able to endure. Tim did see a pair of gentlemen leaning in for a kiss at one point, but he was able to jerk his head quickly away before having a chance to see how far his level of discomfort could be pushed. Tim barely noticed that as he was pulling himself away from the window, jerking his sight from the kissing couple, the bus driver had twitched a bit toward Tim.

The bus cruised ahead further into the district, and Tim became more apprehensive the further they went. His head dodged the sights of the streets rapidly as the bus drove through. Men holding hands began to become overbearingly frequent. Tim's head jolted back on almost a secondly basis now, or at least it seemed to him, as he dodged the sight of watching two grown, consenting men kiss in public. He didn't mind watching a couple lesbian couples making out on a street corner or two, but the one time he accidentally saw a comparable maneuver performed by a pair of men, it was all he could do to keep from vomiting. Every hug between two men made him shudder, every pair of hands held made him antsy, every kiss made him want to leave his skin, and every rainbow flag seemed to hang in mockery of all that was proper for the world to be. As he grew ever more rigid, if that was possible, with every hug sighted and pair of hands held, he noticed that the driver would show a similar, though incredibly more subtle, reaction of some sort; a twitch, a low moan, a shake of his head.

After ten minutes or so riding around and through the Castro/Mission district, the bus was coming to Market Street. Knowing this, Tim began to relax ever so slightly at the prospect of not having to be surrounded by such filth and wrongness any longer. The bus turned, and much to his dismay and horror, he found that the bus had just put itself in the middle of San Francisco's annual gay pride parade. He suddenly found himself surrounded by floats, colors, men and women in bright, happy costumes covered in sequins, and other costumes revealing more than some would deem strictly appropriate for all occasions. He found himself trying to cope with a circumstance altogether unexpected and was suddenly unable to process the data streaming past his eyes and flowing through his head in any sort of coherent, intelligible capacity. Put simply, he now felt himself overload at the sudden shock of being where he was. After several seconds of pure horror trying to reconcile his mind to his eyes to his perspective of the nature of things, he had an even more terrifying thought: what if Hell for him was to be brought to the center of the city he most loved, only to be fucked up the ass by gay faggots the rest of eternity? Considering thus, Tim crouched down on the floor into something resembling a vertical fetal position. He closed his eyes and began rocking slowly back and forth while humming to himself the first song that came to his mind, the Star-Spangled Banner.

The bus driver turned and looked down at him, giving him something of a funny look. The bus driver then inquired in a queer, half-sincere half-mocking tone of concern, "What, pray tell, are you doing, *boy*?"

Tim didn't seem to hear the bus driver, or, at the very least, simply didn't answer the driver's question. The bus driver posed his question a second time, this time a little bit louder, but still he received no answer. Finally, the bus driver raised his voice significantly louder, though without any change to his strange tone, and asked him a third time to explain his behavior. To this third posing of the exact same question, Tim glanced up at the driver with a scowl on his face, and in a shaky voice uttered almost inaudibly, "Can't take it. People like these . . . the . . . these corruptors of nature and everything normal and have no reason or place to exist . . . they shouldn't be . . . and I can't take it!" Tim finished on a louder note than when he had begun.

The bus driver looked down at him crouching practically under his seat, fears contorting his face in the strangest ways, betraying feelings of vileness and sheer contempt. As slowly a warm smile rose to the bus driver's face, he responded to Tim with a sort of joviality in his voice, "And I suppose you think that squatting in fear and making a pretzel out of your face at the first sign of some vibrant costumes is completely normal? Regardless, I was informed by a bird or two that you were no happier in life than when in this city, and you were supposed to be enjoying this pre-Hell ride. You obviously don't care for the city as much as I was given the impression, however, so rather than torture you any further, I'll have you out of this place in a jiff and riding through some country perhaps a little bit more to your liking."

As promised, it was a matter of only seconds before the driver turned the bus down the next street and away from the parade. As the bus turned, like the parting of the Red Sea, the cops seemed to automatically know to separate the barricades dividing the spectators from the parade, and the crowd split before the bus and closed behind it after it had passed through. The bus now headed toward Golden Gate Park.

After traveling another two or three minutes, Tim decided that it would be safe to sit up next to the window again. Ten minutes or so later, they had come to the Golden Gate Bridge. As the bus rolled toward the end of the bridge, Tim found himself beginning to suffer pangs of regret that he wasn't able to see any more of the city that he had held so close to his heart for so long. He looked backwards toward the city for as long as he could, feeling a loss that he slowly realized perhaps he could have even for a short time put off, had he not been so anxious. But then, he reminded himself, it was probably far better to have gotten out of the sheer torture he had found himself in and leave the closest thing to Heaven he had ever known than to stay and harm himself further. He sighed bittersweet as the bus left the city behind.

———

Save for a touch of lingering regret he couldn't seem to shake, Tim was actually able to relax himself far more fully than he had been while in the city. It had taken a good ten minutes or so once out of view of the cityscape to calm himself again, but now he felt as though only one set of his muscles were tense rather than two; a marked improvement from before.

Shortly after Tim's said moment of relaxation, the bus driver, with uncanny timing, began to speak. "So skipper, the boys upstairs told me that you really loved the city and that a cruise through it for a while might be a good way to ease your nerves during this . . . time of transition. What got your goat back there that you decided to blow a gasket and have the ol' proverbial meltdown?"

Becoming edgy again at the driver's question Tim slowly responded with a hint of aggravation, "I already told you back there, I just can't stand those fu— . . . those . . . those damned gays!"

"Not to burst your bubble, sonny boy," responded the driver in a tone half quizzical, half jolly, "but they didn't looked like the damned ones from where I was sitting." The driver stared at Tim with a penetrating smirk on his face while his hands easily steered the bus around a bend in the road.

"Look," Tim was more than a little on edge now, "I told you before, it . . . they . . . it just isn't natural, and that rubs me the wrong way."

"Actually," responded the driver, "I remember exactly what you said before. I believe that you mentioned not only that you felt homosexuality was not natural, but that homosexuals are 'corruptors of nature and everything normal,' and that homosexuality has 'no reason or place to exist.' Unless of course I'm mistaken?"

"Hey, you apparently work for God, don't you?" Tim was becoming more agitated by the moment. "What of it? You tell me!" A moment after saying this, Tim realized he might have inadvertently been a bit hasty and arrogant in his response to the guy driving him to Hell.

"Well," the driver responded with his eyes now primarily on the road, looking back toward Tim every so often for emphasis. "For starters, I couldn't help but notice that you weren't disturbed too greatly by those who you accuse of being 'corruptors of nature' being a pair of kissing *women*." Tim grew a little red in the face and was further agitated as the driver noted his observation. The driver continued to speak in a cool manner, both matter of fact and jovial, "As far as male homosexuality goes, you're right. I *do* know God a little bit better, it seems, than you. So, I'll be more than happy to alleviate your confusion, since you've asked so nicely. Perhaps you don't fully consider this when you're thinking about the world around you, but, and let me remind you that your mind can't even begin to grasp these notions in such a way that you may even begin slightly to understand them, as far as you're concerned, God is the *reason* for all that is brought into creation, and therefore, brought into being. God is responsible for every atom, every twig, every blade of grass, every planet, every cosmos, every queer, and every smart-ass condemned to Hell. That's the *nature* of God, you see; *he* brings into being *exactly* what she feels She needs to keep the universe running as He sees fit. No more, no less. This being *God's* nature, neither homosexuals nor the over-quick-to-judge Hell-bound, nor anything else in this universe, of which the Earth, lest you forget, is a rather miniscule piece, is capable of *anything* short of being natural. And further, by these same elementary principles, there is *nothing* that can corrupt the 'normal' and 'natural', since *every* manifestation is natural, and therefore, normal.

"Now, as far as a reason and place to exist go, well . . . It should be obvious even to you that everything inhabits some *place*, and so, let's chalk that part of your statement up to bad wording on your part and a half-assed snide response on mine, shall we?" At which point the driver looked over his shoulder with a warm smile on his face, and for a brief moment Tim, upon seeing the likeness of his father smiling at him, let himself relax. Quickly remembering where he sat and why, however, Tim became almost as tense, though not quite as he had been a moment before, and the driver, whose eyes were now on the road again, continued to speak. "As far as reason goes, well, as I said before, God has 'reasons' for everything from the smallest quark to the largest supercluster of galaxies and everything beyond and below. Your level of focus being as myopic as any common human, it seems you need the obvious pointed out to you; namely that in this case the true topic of question isn't the reason of the existence of homosexuality on *this* planet, but the *cause*. The difference, you see, is that the reason for all phenomena in the universe, objectively speaking, is the same. And the knowledge of that reason belongs solely to what in ignorance you have no better word for than 'God,' as well as those very blessed who *experience directly* that knowledge.

"Since cause, then, becomes the question, to the question of cause I will give an answer." Tim's interest began to waver at this point, and he began to relax himself in the manner of one about to be subjected to a boring, pointless, and rather irritating lecture. It was just as his mood began to change thus that the bus driver's tone of voice changed from uplifting and light to suddenly harsh and almost chastising. Noticing this quick change in the driver's tones of voice, his ears immediately perked up anew as the driver continued. "You see, what you are apparently completely oblivious to is that some percentage of these people whom you are so quick to judge as corruptors were battered and abused until the only way they could continue to tolerate living was to take up the lifestyles they now hold. Some are the genetic result of a brother marrying a sister. Some are the genetic results of two heterosexual people with 'normal' upbringings whose blood is being introduced to each other for the first time since the dawn of time. Some are confused by a confusing world in which they have never had guidance to remedy their confusion, and thus they grope to find love any way they can. Some want to share as much love as they can with *anyone* they can, because what feels better than sharing love? Some have a minor hormonal imbalance that alters their sense of attraction from conforming to what small-minded dolts might typically consider 'normal.' Some seek kindred souls regardless of what face or genitalia it entails. Some love the one it feels most right for them to love, just because it feels right and is right by any and every criteria that could possibly matter to any objectively thinking being. And some," and here the driver's tone became more jovial again with a slight hint of mockery, "God put in place just to screw with the foundations of your poorly built belief system."

At this point the bus driver's voice shifted again, this time to the tone of voice most closely described as his "regular" tone. "Look, partner, the point *is*, there's a 'cause' or 'reason' for everything. I could give you a long-winded lengthy lecture about the laws governing every manifestation in the universe and quickly lose you in some very sophisticated rabble about sevens and threes, but the simple fact of the matter is that even if I could keep your interest for more than eight seconds, you wouldn't be able to understand me much past the ninth. So, how about I give you the 'Reader's Digest' version of how God works, so to speak? It all basically boils down to something one of the wiser beings of your planet wrote a short while ago. If memory serves me right, and it's never done anything but for as long as I've had it, I believe the sentiment goes, 'All is coincidence! One thing begets another.'"

Tim spent a moment attempting to fully take in and assess all he had just heard. He felt in part disquieted and disjointed, in part awed. In part he felt as though he may have just learned something very important, but didn't quite know what to make of it yet. In part he felt strangely detached, as though what he had just heard he had no place to hear. Coupled with all of these odd feelings floating through him was the idea that he had just been fed a crock, and that this image of his father driving him to Hell may well have been talking out his ass.

In part, Tim saw his fears of homosexuality as silly, self-induced, pointless and destructive. This part of him was suddenly a bit angered that he had apparently sacrificed his last chance for the rest of eternity to see the place in the world he loved best, to temporarily feel better about something that he probably shouldn't have flipped out about to begin with. Another part of him felt as though there was some much greater lesson to be grasped that for some reason was for the moment out of his reach. The last part of him thought that the driver was completely full of shit and wanted to resist, deny, and ignore all of what the driver had just said to him. Being the most dominant parts due to the fact that it was these parts irritating him the most, his ignorance, or rather his lack of a fuller picture, coupled with his desire not to know, triggered his response of asking the bus driver, "So what's your point? Are you trying to tell me some 'profound' notion about how the universe works, or is this just your round-about way of telling me I should like fags?"

Tim having asked his question, the bus driver pressed down hard on the gas pedal, shifted gear, and the new momentum of the bus pushed him back stiffly against his seat. For the brief moment before he blacked out, he couldn't move his head to look at anything aside from the big windshield of glass at the front of the bus. In it he could swear that he could make out some large, round, white object next to the driver in the reflection, but for the life--or death, as it seemed at the time--of him, he had no idea what to make of it.

For a brief moment he perceived no light, and yet it seemed to him only an imperceptible moment of darkness had passed over him when suddenly he was looking out at the most amazing sight his gaze had ever beheld.

Looking out through the front window of the bus, he witnessed before him a sight of pure marvel and awe. Galaxies spun everywhere he looked in a black, endless void; a view he had not just in the front window, but in every window he dared to turn his head toward. The universe stretched out before him in a way it never had before and humbled him to his inner-most being. As he began slowly to float from his seat, he found himself wishing as he had never wished before to have his feet firmly planted on the soil of his native planet.

The driver looked at him with sincerity in his eyes and said, "This is the point. This is the reason every atom exists. This is the reason every blade of grass exists. This is the reason every twig exists. This is the reason every 'queer' exists. And, this is the reason that even one condemned and as lowly as you, exists. The point is that should any snail sliming its way down your sidewalk not have been created in the way it was, this could not exist as it does.

"The point is," continued the driver, "that you say to a servant of a being a bit more privy than *you* that your excuse for being mired in fear over a manifestation of God, is that that manifestation goes against the God that created it! The point is that the harm you cause yourself for no *good* reason could easily be avoided if you would merely accept what can't be changed; accept discomfort at being around those of no less value than you, even though *you* may be made a bit uncomfortable because you find yourself unable to accept something you are presently unable to understand. The point is that since no great harm comes from passing through a street that allows you a chance to examine something of a foreign world, you might as well relax and enjoy, if nothing else, some really snazzy costumes. The point is, Tim, instead of making something 'groovy' out of the last sights you may ever see again, you curl into a fetal position lest you see what by your judgment constitutes an 'inappropriate' expression of love, which, objectively speaking, does not exist."

Those final words leaving the bus driver's lips, the driver changed gear again, and a bright light filled Tim's eyes. When his vision returned and he was able again to perceive objects, he found that the bus was heading down a road surrounded by a large Redwood forest.

Book 2
Playing Limbo *With* A <u>Low</u> Bar

Traveling up the 101 towards Oregon, there were great Redwood trees everywhere in front of, as well as on either side of, the bus. After having endured a series of events of a less than settling nature during the course of the day, Tim found himself a bit fatigued. His exhaustion, along with the knowledge that there was no fighting whatever was to come, altogether combined with the pure beauty and serenity of these old, seemingly wise, giant trees completely surrounding him, he was finally able to let himself go. He surrendered himself to relaxation and enjoyed the ride while watching the trees go by. Reflecting upon himself and his past for a moment, it dawned on him that he actually couldn't remember a time having felt quite this good. He knew he'd had enjoyable moments, but he couldn't remember the last time feeling truly as though he just was. He found it incredibly ironic that it was on his way to Hell that he was able to enjoy a feeling so . . . so . . . heavenly.

Hours had passed, and he was in a groove of enjoyment as the bus traveled through the forest. He was sighing in relief when he felt a slight tremble begin somewhere below him under the wheels of the bus.

As the bus rolled on, the earth gradually shook more and more violently. Considering the bus was starting to convulse below them by degrees in a fairly rigorous way, the bus continued at a surprisingly steady, smooth pace. Trees began to rock noticeably due to the thundering quake, and far ahead in the distance, Tim could swear he saw the road begin to rise.

The earth continued to quake with growing intensity, and in the distance the ground seemed to be rising higher and higher. Without slowing, the bus continued down the road, apparently not even noticing the ground undulating below it. Half a minute or so later, Tim was able to see a sort of blackness at the base of the earth rising ahead.

The violence of the tremors in the earth became such that the mammoth trees surrounding them swayed to the brink of falling, and Tim was having extreme difficulty staying in his seat for much more than a couple of seconds at a time. Oddly enough, the bus continued to hug the ground as though it were the last object anchored firmly in a world tearing itself asunder. The risen earth ahead could now be clearly seen, and he saw that what once appeared as a tiny black speck at the bottom of the slowly rising mound, had developed into a huge hole; something of a cave in the earth's risen crust.

The mound of earth gave a final jerk upward and the ground stopped shaking. Tim could see clearly that a second road apparently led *into* the earth. He also now realized how fast the bus was speeding down the highway, and before he had taken the time to fully register their speed, the bus had moved quickly into the very dark tunnel that had arisen from out the earth before him. The earth shook violently again, and it wasn't long before the last shreds of sunlight left his perception. He could feel the hum of the bus continuing to ride along, but the world now surrounding him was one of pure, perfect, darkness.

The floor of the earth having barely ceased its tremors, Tim gasped with a claustrophobic horror as the notion quickly flooded his mind that his eyes would never be touched by the rays of the sun ever again.

As a very young child, he had slept with a nightlight, but he had thought that he had left his fear of the dark behind him long ago. Now he clutched at his seat as beads of nervous perspiration began forming on his brow in response to being shrouded in absolute darkness, able to see absolutely nothing. He perceived only the hum of the motor, the vibration of the bus, and the violent palpitations of his heart. He was seconds away from rolling himself into a familiar ball-like position when out of the darkness a voice pierced through his terror and entered his ears as softly as wind chimes being blown by a gentle morning breeze. "How're you holding up back there, Scout?"

Tim, finding himself now torn between the disparate emotions of gratitude at being able to communicate with someone despite his initial feeling of dissolution, and the feeling of pure terror he couldn't have possibly imagined before today that he was capable of, he attempted to speak.

"Ar-ar-Are . . . are we th-the-there? I . . . I m-mean here. I-I mean . . .Hell?"

In response, the driver gave a soft chuckle and spoke in a reassuring tone. "No, my boy. Actually, we still have quite a ways to go before reaching your destination. This is merely a tunnel. A little dark, I'll grant you, but I actually find it to be one of the more calming, relaxing paths I find myself on from time to time. Don't you?" Tim could swear that he saw the dim flash of a smile upon hearing these last words leave the driver's lips.

Tim found himself able to relax slightly at hearing the driver's words and asked, this time in a much clearer voice, "How long?"

"Well," began the driver, "it doesn't really matter, does it? Here we are in this wonderfully relaxing pitch-black darkness, no sound but the motor, and time is always fleeting. It's really just like the rest of the trip, Tim. Let yourself go and enjoy the moments as you get them. This tunnel is a rare treat that very few souls get to 'see.' Do yourself a favor and enjoy the quiet. Become the darkness, have no thought to your worries, and despite the inevitable, you might just find yourself enjoying the ride."

Tim found himself doing exactly as the driver had suggested. At first, he was still fairly tense and filled with anticipation by thoughts of what might be coming next. After some mere minutes, however, which he could not distinguish now from the passing of hours, he found that he simply no longer had the emotional strength to maintain a high level of anxiety. He surrendered himself to his situation and surroundings and fell into a deep relaxation; a relaxation even deeper than when he had been cruising amidst the trees.

As he began to relax, the notion of getting some sleep entered his mind. He noticed, however, that even after the day he'd had, which would likely be considered tiring by just about any objective measure, he felt absolutely no urge to sleep. Tim remembered the driver saying something earlier about not existing in the physical as far as the "earthly realm" was concerned. He figured this must mean that this sort of newly disembodied version of him didn't need sleep.

With this thought, Tim drifted into a deep relaxation, no longer concerned about the possible needs of his body. He felt as though he were dissolving or blending into the impenetrable black surrounding him. He remained in a profound silence for what felt as though a short eternity had melted by before he was brought back to a more corporeal state of consciousness by the loving voice of his father. "Timmy boy, it's time to open your eyes. You have a short walk to take."

———————

Tim felt a cessation in the vibrations of the bus as the bus driver spoke these words, and he heard the door of the bus open. "Stand up and take my hand, boy." The bus driver said this in a notably stern tone.

Tim was a bit bewildered to find that instinctively he apparently knew exactly where the bus driver's hand was. He simply reached out into the darkness, and his hand found itself directly in the driver's grip. Reaching out, he felt the same sensation he'd experienced when passing closely to another body, a feeling of presence that doesn't need to be confirmed by sight; only this feeling of his hand naturally being drawn to the bus driver was much stronger than similar such feelings he'd experienced. The feel of the bus driver's hand was light and warm, almost as though his own hand was being gripped by a loop of condensed air heated; like the warmth that radiates a few feet from a fire in a fireplace.

"Now make no false move, and do exactly as you are told." The driver spoke grimly and decisively. "There will be exactly three steps down. Be very careful not to lose your footing, and after the third step, keep perfectly still." Tim was beginning to feel himself tense again, but he was reassured by the "grasp" the bus driver had on his hand.

Tim was led forward and instructed that the first step was directly in front of him. He slowly let his right foot descend to the step below. Not surprisingly, his left foot followed his right. Once his feet were again united, his right foot went in search of the second step down. Again came the left foot, and again went the right. As his right foot fell a final time, Tim detected that the ground was softer, perhaps as though made of earth, than the metal step he was stepping off of had been. Down came his left foot. He did not dare move further in the thick blackness that surrounded him, considering well the driver's warning. He felt the bus driver step down next to him and heard the door of the bus close behind him.

As Tim stood staring blankly into the impenetrable darkness permeating all his senses, the bus driver spoke the two most ironic words Tim had ever heard in his life: "Now watch."

Tim stared to his right in the direction of the driver's voice and the warmth he felt beside him. As he looked to the right, at first he saw nothing. Then, in a faint glow, he saw the vague outline of the driver's hand in a pinching position. As the hand drew back, Tim saw the glow grow brighter until he could clearly see a softly glowing ball of light in between the driver's fingers, apparently being withdrawn from out of the darkness. Though he had seen no light since his last glimpse of the end of the tunnel, the little ball barely showing the outline of the driver's hand posed no irritation to his eyes.

The driver held the ball in front of Tim and instructed him to hold it. Tim placed the palm of his hand directly under the ball of light. Once the driver had set the ball upon his hand, he clenched his fist tightly over the ball to make certain that there was no chance of it slipping from his hand. In making certain he had a firm grip on the ball, he effectively stifled the possibility of any light escaping from within his grasp.

The driver's tone changed from firm and cautionary to a tone of sympathy. "I understand that you don't want it to fall, Tim, but what good is the light it gives if you hold onto it so tightly that it cannot be seen by either myself, or probably much more importantly, *you*? Please, be so kind as to open your hand and pinch it between two fingers of your other hand."

Tim was momentarily fearful of this solitary source of light escaping him, but he did as the driver requested.

"Thank you," said the driver. "You see, it is much better to enjoy what you have while you have it, to whatever extent you may, despite the slight risk of losing it, rather than holding onto it so tightly you wind up losing the essence of the very thing which you wished so completely to experience. At times you must even let go entirely, having faith that despite what appears to be a loss, something will appear in your future to fill the void, perhaps to overflowing, that you otherwise would not have received had you not let go when the time came.

"Tim, please be so kind as to extend your arm so that the ball is directly in front of you and as far away from your body as you can hold it."

Tim did as the bus driver told him to do.

"Now let go."

Tim hesitated for a moment. As he stood for that moment in indecision, he felt regret at the prospect of letting go of the simple yet subtly amazing artifact that he now held at his fingertips. Not only was this object something he had never seen anything like before in his life, it was also the first light he had seen in what felt like days, if not years, and certainly the only illumination there was now. Considering this, with an air of regret, he let go.

Tim thought that by letting go, the ball might dissolve into the air. He thought that perhaps it would fall to the ground and break or become dark. He thought that his approach to his current situation might be some kind of test, and that when the ball fell with no more consequence than to land on the ground by his feet, the driver would let out a laughing, "I told you so," and they would get back into the bus and drive on. He was mildly surprised to see his expectations shattered when he dropped the ball and it fell past his feet, and continued falling.

Despite the light being dim, Tim was able to see the glow of the ball continue falling more than a full minute after he had released it. It seemed like many more minutes had passed before the soft illumination had been engulfed completely in the all-consuming pitch black of whatever long drop lay far too close for comfort at his feet. Despite the perfect silence surrounding him, he never did hear the sound of anything hitting a "bottom" to the presumable abyss before him.

He was startled from his deep concentration on the ball's location and the sound of silence that he hoped would be broken any moment by the sound of the ball hitting ground below. The driver's voice again took on a stern tone of admonition. This time it came from his left. "I expect you know full well now why to watch carefully your every step. Take my hand and keep close." He wondered how the driver wound up on the other side of him, but quickly decided the question wasn't worth the pain of pondering as he let his left hand find the driver's and began slowly walking.

The driver led Tim around to the front of the bus. Surprisingly firmly, the driver gripped him by the shoulders and positioned him where he wanted him to stand. The driver released his grip, and in a couple of moments Tim heard the driver's voice coming from slightly ahead. "Follow the light in *exactly* a straight line and it will take you *exactly* where you need to go. The bus cannot travel the path you must now walk on your own, so, we'll meet up with you again on the other side of your journey. You will encounter an old friend of mine toward the end of the route you are about to take. Try not to be too frightened."

Tim again saw the outline of the driver's hand, and again, seemingly from nowhere, a ball of light appeared from out of the darkness. This time, however, it was bigger; fist-sized. The driver dropped the ball to the ground, and the ball began to roll forward. The driver told him to follow, and so he did. As he followed the light rolling forward before him, Tim heard behind him the soft rumble of a motor and the bus driving away.

Save for the speck of light directly in front of him, Tim walked by himself in complete darkness. As he walked, he thought to himself. He thought that the driver's words had been reassuring. He thought, and more importantly felt, that he had very little left to fear in the darkness that stretched infinitely before him. He felt no tiredness from his body at all at this point, and thought that he could walk in this place, what the driver had described as a tunnel, alone for days without exhaustion or worry about what might possibly lie ahead. Tim thought that whatever lay ahead couldn't be too terrible. Then his thoughts shifted to a remembrance that every step he took brought him one step closer to Hell.

But he again remembered the driver's words instructing him not to be frightened, and he remembered that he was still to be driven at the end of this short trek. By remembering what the driver had told him, his nerves were greatly eased. He relaxed further as he remembered the driver's consistent advice to relax and enjoy the journey while he was still on it. So, he strode quickly, leaving his thoughts behind him, and did his best to enjoy his walk.

Tim continued in this state for what felt like he'd been walking a good solid two hours rather than half of one, when suddenly the light began moving ahead more rapidly. A moment or two later, it stopped some way off in the distance. Several minutes of walking later he noticed that the light was getting bigger as he drew nearer, and shortly thereafter he found himself standing in front of a wall composed of dim light exactly the color and brightness of the ball he had been following.

Where he stood, the wall softly illuminated the area surrounding him. He now saw not only no chasm next to his path, but that he seemed to be enclosed on all sides by a large circular room or cave. The path he had taken to enter the room still lay behind him, but otherwise there were no other places to go from this room. Aside from the large, glowing wall that stood facing him, he couldn't tell if there was anything on any of the other walls. They were obscured by shadow.

Curious, he was about to touch the illuminated wall when he heard a voice hiss sharply, though barely audibly, "Get back!" In front of his hand a shape began to appear. He started to walk backward very slowly, filling with a sense of dread.

The shape of a head began to protrude from out of the faint light. Tim stood stock still as he watched the featureless orb mold itself from the subdued radiance. Eye sockets began to depress into the head as the shape of a nose began to extend. Next the outline of a mouth poked out from under the nose; lips expressionless as stone. Eyes filled the eye sockets, and detail by detail the head formed the features of a face complete with every nuance of Tim's hair, ears, forehead, cheekbones and chin, until he was staring eye to eye with an exact replica of his own visage, stuck out of the wall and composed of the one uniform, pale-white glow.

The glow of the wall and the head slowly began to tint. In a matter of seconds the soft, reassuring white light became a dull, sickening shade of green. The eyes in the head on the wall began to bulge, the mouth contorted into a hideous sneer and a long, forked tongue lashed out of its mouth as though trying to strike at him. Its hair became a weave of hundreds of small snakes. Tim started stumbling backward, horrified. He tripped and looked up with sheer terror as arms began to form out of the wall by the head, reaching out toward him.

The head spoke in a shrill hiss. "Get out and go away! You don't belong here."

A second mouth with sharp teeth formed in the wall, not too far from the original hideous head, and began to speak as it became accompanied by large eyes with slits and the rest of its face. "Be gone to the darkness, being of damnation!" An arm appeared by this newly emerging head, pointing outward toward the way Tim had originally come in.

A third mouth of thin, ragged lips and decaying, stench-laden teeth protruded from out the wall, shrilling, "Miscarriage of nature not fit for our sight, be gone! Be gone! Leave!" And long nails began to stick out by this head, long before any hand could begin to be seen attached to them.

And more mouths formed, and more heads and arms followed, much as the first three sets. Ever more heads and arms and mouths and odors and shrill hisses ascending into a chant of wailing in the high pitches joining together. "Out! Out! Out! Out! Out! Out! Out! Out!" Each face more hideous and horrifying than the last. Each eye filled with its own soul-piercing evil. A multitude of arms reaching out further and further toward him, and the faces began to chant, "Let us take it out of our misery, let us cease it damning our sight!"

Tim, chilled stiff with a fear he had never thought he could be capable of, forced himself to his feet, directed himself toward where he had originally come, and ran as fast as he possibly could. He had run no more than nine strides when he felt a very large, bony pair of hands clamp down on his shoulders, lifting him off the ground.

He felt the hands griping his shoulders from the front rather than from behind, but at the moment he was a bit too preoccupied with the all-numbing blood-palpitating hysteria controlling his every action to take note of this minor incongruity. As he was lifted up, he was certain that his next sensation would be being wrenched backward and skinned alive. He closed his eyes and awaited the inevitable, but the outcome he had anticipated never occurred.

After several moments of dangling in midair, Tim, noticing that nothing *yet* had happened, decided, with great reluctance, to open his eyes. He could still hear far too well for comfort a mixture of moaning and hissing coming from the wall behind him. He was also apparently close enough to the wall that the faintest hint of the putrid glow coming off of that wall fell on whatever it was that was now in front of him. He could barely make out a few very large, round, white lines of the shape he faced, but nothing finite in the pale gloom barely offering muted light.

Tim heard a scratchy voice, rough and very loud, speak from the darkness directly in front of him. "The laws of this realm state that I must show myself to thee before shall be I able to speak thee what thou hast need to know afore progressing onward. But you may be forewarned, though in this instance I am to aid you and not bring you oblivion, though in this instance be I friend and not foe, some would find my form displeasing. And so I warn thee that thou might find ease in me and not dismay." These words having been spoken, flame ignited atop two large torches, warming either side of Tim's face. Seeing what apparently the source of the voice had been, he let fly from his throat a shriek louder and longer than any he had let loose before in his life.

———————

Tim wanted to faint, but his apparent lack of "non-earthly physicality" seemed to prevent him from the ability to lose direct consciousness. He wanted to shut his eyes, but the fire of the flames was apparently not the typical fire he had known on the surface of the Earth and readily pierced through what he thought were his eyelids, forcing him to look at the ghastly visage staring him in the face despite his eyes being technically shut. He wanted to direct his gaze elsewhere, but he found himself frozen solid with fear, and just closing his eyelids took every ounce of what little concentration he had been able to muster; and besides that, it was too big. He was too paralyzed to turn his head, and no movement of his eyes could have caused him to look at anything that was not what was now facing him eye to blood-dripping, maggot-filled, cobra-pupiled eye.

Just to look at *one* of its two boulder-sized wriggling eyes was blood-freezing enough, but the unfortunate fact was that these were only a small detail of this monstrous face facing Tim. It was a skull, giant, white, and humbling if just for its size alone; never mind its composition. On the top of the skull were slugs, snails, and worms five times larger than any he had ever seen, sliming around a sort of dripping, boiling fungus crawling with spiders of all different colors, shapes and sizes. It was as though the top of its head was alive with a living, crawling, slimy hair dripping and slipping and dangling around and down its scalp. Its pupils turned their hissing heads, staring at him, at times trying to strike and being just out of reach of his face. Around the corners of its eyes were mounds of dried, rust-colored blood and puss that looked as though it had been forming for centuries, with fresh, thick red trickling down amongst it. From out of its nose crawled and fell an occasional slug or twenty from its head and dripped down its upper lip bone and into its mouth, a thick, black, somewhat lumpy liquid-like substance. Its teeth were like moldy shards of glass, and blood streamed from rank, black mounds of what vaguely resembled gums holding the teeth in place. Its tongue was reminiscent of two sides of beef that had been festering in this thing's mouth since the world had been conceived. The stench that arose from this thing had not been present until the torches were lit, heating the air. Tim was certain that had his body been "earthly physical," it would have shriveled to raisin size due to the permeating odor alone, which was utterly suffocating and ungodly sickening. He found his body unable to vomit, but every muscle contracted within him wanting to. Its hands were refreshing compared to the rest of it; just long, clean, bleach-white bones of arms and hands extending far, though not far enough, from either side of it, holding him firmly and unwaveringly in midair. There was a little blood and puss under its fingernails, but he wouldn't really be aware of that fact until after it released him. And besides, at this moment the putrid stench, sight, and cobras constantly striking close to his cheeks held his attention far more persistently than thoughts of the cleanliness of this being's hands.

He continued to scream and scream. When this thing facing him began to speak once more, he gave no indication that he was going to stop his blood-curdling shrieks any time in the near future. The gargantuan face spoke in the same scratchy tone it had before, though this time it was far louder than it had previously been. "**SILENCE!**"

This blast of sound, coupled with the actual hearing of the command and the unbearable stench that wafted up about him as the creature's voice vibrated the air violently surrounding him, quickly put a halt to his initial high-pitched protests. He screamed no more, and felt that there was nothing left to do at this point but hang in this thing's bony grip, paralyzed with fear at the sight of what was before him.

"Wasn't thou warned of what thou wast walking toward?" spoke the skull, the putrid scent barraging Tim's nostrils almost visible as various forms of green-black slime and slugs dripped around and down its teeth.

Tim found himself unable to move his mouth in reply.

"**SPEAK!**" commanded its morbidly massive mouth.

"H-h-h-ha-ha-he," began Tim, focusing any will power and concentration he could muster to his mouth muscles, "Hi-hi-he s-s-sai-sai-id ne-ne-nn...not tt-ttt-to b-b-bb-b-b-b-be fa-fa-fa-fa-fri-t-t-end."

If it was possible, and from where Tim was hanging that was a pretty big if, the two globes of maggots that made up the thing's eyes seemed to look affectionately upon him. As close to tenderly as something the likes of which it was could. It spoke, "These words told to thee are wise. You would do well to heed them. Thou shall not be harmed by me *this* meeting."

Tim looked at the cobras extending from its eyes; he swore that for a brief moment he saw their fangs disappear. He continued to maintain a fairly consistent level of frozen-stiffness at the sight of the revolting thing that was before him, but his feelings of immediate peril were, at least temporarily, assuaged. He found now more than enough strength to give three half-nods of his head in acknowledgment.

With an air thick and rank, the skull continued, "Thy path lies from thou dids't just come."

Tim's feeling of immediate peril returned.

The cobras looked over him as though scanning his face, and again it spoke, "To walk through the illusion of affliction, of death; to let thy self die, and in so doing, come to life, this is to see the light. Thy path is straight and lies from where thou hast come. Continue forward at any pace and thou shall come to light in thy pace's due time. Stop and you will be frozen, unable again to move, and thus, perhaps, forever lost."

Tim hung, still quite frozen with fear, and now, with a dumbfounded look on his face. The cobras looked deeply into his eyes, their bodies gesticulating back and forth. Looking, somehow, into all four eyes at once, he felt suddenly transparent, as though something very great was looking through him, seeing every nuance of him completely. He felt he had no secrets, as though every aspect of his being was completely known. At first, he felt shame. It was like being viewed in full nakedness by total strangers passing by, some stopping to stare indefinitely. Quickly, however, this shame gave way to a different feeling, new, odd. He felt liberated. He felt that he could hide nothing, but that he had no need to. He felt as though there was no cause for feeling shame; he felt as though there was no malice behind the eyes examining him. In fact, he even felt a sort of kindness, a . . . light, motivating that which watched him.

The cobras broke their gaze with Tim as they returned to their previous state of undulation back and forth, occasionally striking out at him. He felt no longer *seen*.

He did his best to shake his head "no."

"Before you are to enter your Hell," it spoke, "you are to see Heaven."

Tim felt slightly warm and relieved by this statement, but found himself now completely bewildered.

"I am, you see, the keeper, and you ran from *my* gate."

Tim had a strong feeling about what he was about to hear next, and he really didn't want his hunch confirmed. His suspicions were, unhappily, all too quickly verified.

"I am the keeper, oh Hell-bound, of the gates thou hast run from; the gates of Heaven. These gates prevent the damned from entrance to that realm where they do not belong. I am here so that the damned may not return. You are an exception, however. You are to glimpse Heaven before thou dost enter thine own Hell. So, now my job becomes to guide ye thus. Walk now through my gates that thou may see what thou hast need and have been chosen to see."

It lowered Tim to the ground. Upon being released from its grasp, he just stood where he had been set down; staring at the skull, petrified with fear, utterly confused, and without any notion of what at this point he should, if anything, be doing. He thought about returning to the wall of demons this thing claimed as being the gates of Heaven. He also thought about running back into the darkness from where he had come to escape his more immediate fears.

As if in answer to his thoughts, the eyes of the skull suddenly burst into flame and it blaringly screeched, "**WALK HITHER**," the Gatekeeper seemed now to grow, dwarfing Tim even more than it already had, "**LEST I FORGET MY ORDERS AND CLOSE MY GATE TO THEE PERMANENTLY, INTRODUCING THEE TO OBLIVION AS I WOULD ANY OTHER HELL-BOUND!**"

Tim felt his legs carry him at once as quickly as they could toward what in his previous experience had been the, in retrospect no longer so terrifying, wall of demonic souls. He ran in desperation in order to escape the horrible sound of the Gatekeeper's voice. He ran to escape the terrible air-engulfing reek that had emitted from its unfathomably rank mouth. He ran to escape the fate, whatever that may be, of all other Hell-bound who were *not* allowed to traverse the gates of Heaven.

As he ran, he felt as though he was fueled by a fire, one ironically soul-freezing to behold.

Then, as he was about to touch the putrid-green wall he had come to before, he stopped dead in his tracks. As he was running, he hadn't thought much about how horrible the demonic forms in the wall who seemingly had tried to devour him had been. As he approached this second time, Tim saw no sign of them and the wall again was a pale white, as it had begun the last time he was here. Now in very close proximity, within arms reach of the wall, again he saw the old sickly hue of green return and a head begin to surface. Halting his movement forward at the first sign of what he knew would soon follow, he began slowly to back away.

Heads begat faces writhing in agony, and long, slender hands with long nails began reaching out of the wall toward Tim. The demonic forms yowled in anguished tones of torture as they began teasing and taunting Tim with renewed threats of bringing about his swift annihilation.

Tim continued slowly backing away, and did so with confusion and hesitation. As he backed away he remembered what the Gatekeeper had told him about this being the gates of Heaven, but he didn't understand how this could be possible. He remembered what the Gatekeeper had told him about illusion, but nothing could be more real to him at that moment than the horror he felt permeating his being. He remembered what the Gatekeeper had said about death, but death wasn't exactly his fear so much as pain.

Then, he shocked himself by deciding to act in a way he never expected himself to act. He stopped backing away and extended his hand toward the nearest outreached claw. He found himself testing the substance of his own being as he tested the substance of what appeared to be certain death staring him in the face and stretching toward him. He remembered the Gatekeeper's words as he extended his finger toward the hand of what appeared to be an anguished, demonic soul. He felt a spark deep within his being the likes of which he had never felt before. It felt as though a small pinprick of strength and calm was standing alone inside of him, barely warming him and surviving against the raging storm winds of frostbiting terror turning every which way throughout his person.

His finger met with that of the "soul," and sure enough, passed straight through it like a stick through a small stream of smoke. He did notice, however, that when he had touched this apparition the finger had felt ice-cold, and this single touch chilled him to the bone. At this sensation, he remembered the Gatekeeper's words about freezing if he should stop and realized just how literal this statement must have been. He hesitated for a moment, then acted.

Tim backed up three steps, took a very deep breath, and ran forward. As he ran through, the wall was disrupted as when an airplane flies through a cloud, causing the "souls" to lose their form and leave a vacancy where he passed through.

Focused on moving forward, he perceived only by his periphery the vacancy fill and close behind him. He didn't dare look back.

Tim began his run at a good, strong pace. He was completely surrounded by mists of the same pallid, sickeningly greenish hue that had colored the "wall of souls." As he ran through this green-tinged world of mist, shadow, and fear, he swore that he could almost, just barely, feel something, or someone, lightly grasping at his ankles. This sensation of being grabbed at caused him to stumble in his run every several paces or so.

His gait was strong as he began his run, but he was surrounded by an eerie coldness that on the one hand apparently was kept from affecting him by his continuous motion, but on the other gradually slowed him, sapping his stamina and causing him to have to work twice as hard as he otherwise might have in order to keep his energy up. He expected to get tired, but the cold seemed to cause loss of vigor at almost double the rate his running normally would have. The feeling of something grabbing at him became stronger as he ran further.

The green world around him slowly seemed less green and brightened as he kept running, but the mists surrounding him were still far less than friendly. The feeling of being grabbed at diminished slightly with the diminishing of the green hue, but while these feelings of being tugged at were gradually lessening, as he slowed, so too were they strengthening.

Tim didn't know if he had been running a quarter hour or a full hour as he perceived his surroundings were far lighter than they had been when he first began. They were, however, still unfriendly and foreboding. The grabs at his ankles were infrequent, but now they were strong. He felt a definite grip around his ankle that took a significant tug to pull away from. Seconds later he felt an even stronger grip and, breaking away from *it*, he lost his right shoe. He thought about stopping to retrieve it, but without a pause in his stride quickly thought better. He continued running forward, not wanting to be lost to these mists and whatever it was trying to hold him back.

Time sped by as wisps of vapor while Tim ran slowly but consistently. The atmosphere around him was more pleasant than not, the mists being only a light shade of green, not happy, but not entirely unpleasant either. The grabs at his feet were infrequent, but by now he had lost his other shoe to something attempting to stifle subsequent footfalls. Every hold he felt around his ankle, or on his heel, or his toes, took significant force to pry loose from. He felt more certain that he wouldn't have the energy to get loose unless he stopped every time something's grip tried to falter his step. At moments such as these, the words of the Gatekeeper rang clear in his mind, "Stop and you will be frozen . . . forever lost."

Time hung heavy as hours held in each moment he moved through the mists as he found himself slowed significantly since he had begun. The vapors encapsulating him were almost pure-white in color, but an unbearable cold permeated the air around him. He didn't feel anything pulling on him at the moment, and the last time he could remember having felt like something grabbed at him was hours if not days, or perhaps minutes, beforehand. He knew that maybe the reality was it had been only a fraction of any of these measures of the passing of perception prior to the moment he was now experiencing.

While he couldn't imagine himself maintaining any kind of pace like he had been for more than half of an hour, simultaneously it felt like he had been running for days. His feet felt heavy, forward movement became difficult, and the cold surrounding him cooled him deeper and deeper to his core.

Tim grew slower with every step. His thoughts began to fade in and out; he was barely able to think. He tried to remember how long he had been running, if one could call what he now did running, but he no longer had any conception of time. He knew it couldn't have possibly been less than fifteen minutes, but on the other hand it felt as though he had been moving himself forward by sheer will alone through this infinite expanse of mist for years. All he knew was that he was terribly tired, that he was barely able to think enough to tell himself that he was tired, and that he certainly couldn't contemplate how long it had taken him to become this tired. Fading in and out of his own thoughts, he felt finally as if he had been running since the dawn of creation.

As time wore down his spirit and froze him closer and closer to his central-most self with each passing moment, his "run" had become scarcely more than a wholehearted stumble toward what he blindly hoped would be an imminent cessation to his suffering. As time wore on, and his mind slowly failed him, it was only occasional flashes of the words made by the Gatekeeper's voice, "Frozen . . . Forever lost," that kept him moving forward at all. The world became brighter and was almost pure white; nothing had grabbed at him for some time. He knew that if he could go just a little bit farther, the mists must end, and he could rest.

So Tim pressed himself forward. He was cold, he needed rest; he felt fatigue washing over him like waves pushing the sand on a beach. But the world around him was white and pure and nothing grabbed at him. The air felt no longer thick as it had when he had begun through the mist, but light and soothing. But the tiredness plagued him; the fires of fear and will that had pushed him expediently onward when he had started were cooled down to the center of his being by the world around him, and he now could barely drag himself along.

He had spent a great deal of time petrified with fear of leaving any gap in his movements, but now he had no choice but to succumb to the cold as he stumblingly walked, barely able even to do that much. The tired had all but won and the inevitable struck at him like a frosty hammer. There was simply nothing that could allow him to move further. He tried to urge his body forward, but his body tensed with cold and exhaustion. He took one step, two steps, three steps and his arms spread out before him, his eyes closed, and he fell forward toward the ground.

He anticipated something as he fell, but he didn't know quite what. He thought briefly that at worst he would freeze at any point during his fall, remaining motionless where he froze for eternity. This fear, however, entered and left his head within the time frame of a ten-thousandth of the lifespan of a spark of an electron, for the truth of the matter was that at this point, he had left not even the energy required to tense a single brain cell in thought for whatever fate may await him.

Tim's hands felt themselves push away something like a curtain as he fell. Indeed, while falling, his hands pushed away the last layers of thick, white mist, which remained like a heavy drape separating him from what lay just beyond. As this last layer of mist was pushed aside, a warm, warm light was revealed that caressed his arms, face, neck and back as he completed his fall forward into the softest, most fragrant flowers he had ever experienced.

Then came a brief flash, and he felt refreshed and awake. He rolled himself over. Smiling, his face against a backdrop of radiant light, was the bus driver, his teeth shinning almost as brightly as the light behind him. "Welcome to Heaven, boy!" rang in Tim's ears.

Book 3

Manifestation 1: The Feel-Dis (this) of (I) Eye-lie (lay)-some

Tim sat up. He was sitting on a small hill covered with brightly colored, fragrant flowers. Surrounding this veritable island of flowers was a sea of vibrant, flowing grass of all different shades of greens and blues. The grass swayed gently back and forth as though being blown by a gentle breeze, which, as far as he could tell, was not present. Now, fairly far behind him, he could see a wall of mist moving further and further away into the distance. A bright light permeated the "sky" of this place and seemed to cause everything to radiate, as though everything was made up of light. About a yard from his right hand stood a large, healthy-looking black and white cow.

He looked at the cow for a moment in disbelief, then stared at the driver with a puzzled look on his face.

The driver smiled and responded to Tim's look. "We want the Indians to feel at home here. Besides, everyone else who arrives here seems to get a pretty big kick out of her, too."

Tim was about to open his mouth to speak when the driver cut him off. "I know, I know. You have more pressing issues on your mind right now then 'What's with the cow?', right?

"The boys upstairs had their doubts that you would make it this far, but I had faith in you."

Tim asked with hopeful wonder, "Does this mean I've earned the right to go to Heaven, then?"

With a warm, kindly smile, the driver responded, "Your fate is to dwell in Hell for a good, long while. That fate cannot be changed but in the earthly realm. No, you've only earned the right to *see* Heaven. Feel privileged, though, most don't even get this much!

"Look kid, you're going to wind up in Hell when this trip is over. There's nothing you can do to change that. You can, however, marvel at the sights to be seen while you are here. All things considered, that's pretty friggin' good, and like I said before, not a chance that just any Hell-bound soul receives. Hey, just the fact that you survived the Gatekeeper and the wall'o'souls is more than just about any other of the Hell-bound can brag about. You should count yourself as fortunate just to see this first of the Heavenly manifestations!"

Tim looked out of confusion, not quite knowing how he should respond to any of what the driver had just said.

The driver began to answer the question that Tim wasn't even fully aware that he was starting to want to ask. "Perhaps you would like to know about where exactly you just were? Come walk with me to the bus and I'll explain along the way. And if you keep on the socks, you're going to miss out on the grass!"

Tim stood up in the flowers. Shuddering for a brief moment as he recalled why his socks were not accompanied by shoes, he removed his socks and did indeed find the grass between his toes had a delightful consistency, strangely not so unlike the wool of sheep. Far in the distance in front of him he saw a small speck against the light of the radiance that shone everywhere that wasn't ground or something on the ground. He and the driver started walking toward *that* speck. The cow turned its head in Tim's direction and gave a long, loud, "MOOOOOOOO," as if to say farewell and wish Tim good tidings. He noted that the moo sounded reminiscent of a great, copious choir that filled the air with an awe-inspiring tone that brought him to a state of profound quiet and gratitude. The *only* way he could describe the sound he heard was, "*ANGELIC*."

––––––––

As Tim walked with the driver he felt the blades of grass bend beneath the soles of his feet. The grass was smooth and soft as he strode across the meadow. He felt happy walking on this warm, soft grass, surrounded by this beautiful iridescence in the air.

As they walked, the driver spoke. "You've probably been told tales of people's 'near death experiences' and heard about their common experience described as the seeing of 'a bright light at the end of a long, dark tunnel,' right?"

Tim nodded in the affirmative.

The driver continued, "Well, you just took the long way down that very same tunnel."

Tim's face was without expression as he waited for the driver to continue.

"So it happens like this," the driver went on. "When a person dies, their soul travels out of their body at damn near the speed of light. *If* Heaven-bound, the soul knows right where to go and makes a bee-line straight through the gates of Heaven when the gate itself is of pure light. That is before the gate has a chance to register a foreign presence and manifest the 'lost souls', and the soul never has to have the hassle of dealing with the Gatekeeper.

"In the case of a 'near death experience,' the soul takes to the notion that the body is dead when the body looks like it's about to degenerate into lower matter, so that the soul won't need to experience all the pain that the body may experience while it is dying. When *thee* soul leaves *the* body before the body has died, it is still attached to the body via a very fine substance. For the sake of conversation, we'll call this substance 'spiritual string.' When the body dies, *this* string is cut, and the soul goes wherever it's going to go. *Now*, if the body does not die, the string kind of tugs the soul back, and upon awakening, a person may retain some memory of the tunnel, which they can later share with Oprah and the rest of the world.

"In some cases, it takes a while for the soul to return to the body, or the body for whatever reason may not be in a state appropriate for housing the soul, temporarily or otherwise. This will often manifest in the case of a variety of states, most often these states being associated with what you would call 'comas.' In the case that a person doesn't come out of *this* state, often it is because the soul has already moved too deeply into its after-death, and the connection to the body is snapped, leaving an empty body and a soul that has been freed and feels no need to return.

"Now, in the case of one *not* bound for Heaven, one of several things may occur. A person might instantly come back to earth to complete the work that they were supposed to have done by the time of their death.

"Certain souls are known as being 'lost.' Once *their* bodies die, these souls cannot see the light, and so fall from the path in the tunnel where they fall in darkness, usually, forever. *At the point of the fall of the soul*, the soul is *not* a soul. That is to say, during life, the soul was somehow transformed through darkness to become only of the darkness and cannot find its way to the light again. Once the soul falls, it is no longer a soul, it is merely lost, it is void, it is nothing, *and 'it' is what 'it' is*. Really, it's damn near impossible to describe with words, which are always ever so lacking, so, let's just say that for all intents and purposes, they are those who strayed too far and are ultimately lost from any connection with anything, and therefore of no further use to the universe. They exist in the non-realm and await the divine rebirth when they may be resurrected to again serve in the cosmic cycle, to again have purpose. They are lost, but not forgotten, for in the greatest picture, all is and forever will be, All in the One. But again, this cannot mean but little to you since words really become meaningless in *Its* description, so, if you'll excuse me, I'll no longer dwell on that bit of what for you must be something of a headache, and will go on describing the different journeys of the various forms of beings of who-man.

"Now, some-times *it* happens that a lost soul stumbles down the path to actually arrive at the gates of Heaven. Generally, the Gatekeeper catches these Hell-bound souls, reveals himself to them, and eats them."

At this point Tim's face registered a severe expression of shock and intense fear while recalling what the Gatekeeper looked like and pondering that under any other circumstance, he would have been *eaten*.

The driver continued, "I see the *horror* on *your* face, but you must try to understand that such a circumstance is often a blessing, for light is revealed to the soul and the keeper cleanses a dark soul, thereby making it suitable for return to the earthly realm for another shot at life. Granted, however, this is probably also the least pleasant end a soul can come to. One usually has to seriously piss-off one of the highest 'divine beings' to be eaten by the Gatekeeper.

"Often, the Gatekeeper merely reveals himself and the soul plunges back into the darkness from whence it came, inevitably falling from the path and into the void.

"It is said that if a lost soul can find its way to the gates of Heaven and look upon the Gatekeeper with *fearless* eyes, it has *true faith*, and the *fires* that illuminate the Gatekeeper will *cleanse* the soul of its *darkness*, making it ready to enter immediately through the gates of Heaven. But . . . hasn't happened yet . . ." and the driver paused with a fat grin resting on his face.

The driver continued, "Then there are the lost souls that somehow get past the Gatekeeper and *actually* find their way to the gates of Heaven. This is a very rare occurrence, but it does happen. At this point, the 'wall of souls' does *their* thing. Some see the souls and run back into the darkness of oblivion. Some stand petrified in fear in front of the souls and are frozen, then consumed by them, into them, so as to become one *with* them. The *ballsiest* of the Hell-bound actually try to go through. Those who go *through* always do so with a high degree of *ego-induced haughtiness*, and so are *easily tripped down* or otherwise frozen in the fog of the lost. It is said that if **one** were *ever* to find their way through the fog, the light of Heaven would cleanse *that* soul and make it worthy for future existence. *It* has *never* happened . . .

"And no, you didn't get here on your own merits. Hell will still be waiting for you when you get off the bus for the final time."

The driver gave Tim a look suggesting that he had committed a rudeness for even *considering* thinking such a thing, and then continued to speak. "Generally, souls aren't lost. At worst, often they simply haven't completed their assigned work by the end of their lives, and so, need to return to the earthly realm of suffering and coarse labor until they complete what they have need to complete."

As the driver finished his explanations of the different paths various souls take back to Earth or Heaven or what the driver termed "oblivion," Tim looked around the beautiful green, blue-green field upon which he walked. He saw others walking along the grass. He saw people doing summersaults and dancing to the cow's occasional mooing, which could still be heard quite vividly even at a very great distance. He saw people laughing and smiling and talking with each other while standing or sitting. He saw people lying in the grass looking up at the "sky." He saw couples making love freely in the flowing fields. He saw elderly men doing handstands and babies conversing with adults. He saw people flying freely in the air. He saw folk wrestling and playing and enjoying in every form they could think to the beauty of the place that surrounded them. And he saw that there were many, many people sitting all over the fields apparently meditating in lotus positions. He saw some of these people stand up every so often and begin walking in the same direction he and the driver were walking. He enjoyed the beauty of these soft flowing fields, and took great delight in all he saw around him. But most importantly, the place he was **RIGHT NOW**, seemed to stretch on into infinity and every direction thereof, and there seemed to be infinite people in *THIS* place, though *EVERY* being *HE SAW* had **APPARENTLY EXACTLY** the room they wanted to do *WHATEVER* made them feel good, and Happy, and *RIGHT*.

One thing he saw that struck him as odd, even in the place he **NOW FOUND HIMSELF** walking, were many, many people on their hands and knees eating the grass of the field, much as he would expect to see a cow grazing. As he looked up to the driver to enquire, the driver looked warmly at him and said very simply, "Try a blade yerself *child*." Tim bent down, picked a blade of grass and stuck it in his mouth. He was astounded to find that before he began to chew his mouth was filled with the flavor of the most succulent fried chicken he had ever tasted in his life. He swallowed, immediately picking a second blade of grass, and found that this one was like a divine Caesar salad. He picked a theard blade, and enjoyed rich and creamy yogurt-covered raisins.

The driver began to speak again. "Now, you are not exactly just a soul at the moment, so, before we go on, I will describe to you the difference between you and those whom you will be seeing. Most of those who *you* see are those enjoying the first manifestation and making their ways toward subsequent manifestations. Those you see sitting on the grass around you cross-legged, I tend to refer to as the souls who are *truly* lost. Some of these are souls still tethered to the earthly plane in the deepest levels of meditation. In my opinion, they are the truly gifted whom from Earth have mastered themselves so as to be able to experience the first manifestation of Heaven. It would be wise to take note that of the billions of people dwelling on Earth, at the most only a couple of thousand, if that, have been able to conceive to this level from the earthly realm at any *given* point *in* time.

"I say that the **rest** meditating are the *truly* lost because here they are in the first manifestation, and they're meditating instead of experiencing. Some will actually be able to meditate themselves into further manifestations, and so not all who come here and meditate waste the gift they've been given to frivolous forms of concentration of being; but most will merely sit in that position until they finally decide that its time to **open** their **eyes** to the Heavenly **light** and attempt a more **practical** mode of moving **forward**.

"Now, to one of the rare 'Earthers' currently dwelling here, this place is *very* abstract. In fact, to those no longer dwelling in 'their' bodies, this place is slightly more abstract than it appears to you now. For those for whom this is an afterlife, this place can appear very different from being to being. It should be noted, however, that upon arriving **here** after life, the **_COW_** appears to all.

"Your perceptions in this place are directly affected by what you are currently composed of. So, for the sake of some hint of understanding on your part, I will *now* explain *exactly* what at the *moment* you are.

"At your core is what is commonly referred to as your 'soul.' Your soul is the finest gradation of barrier containing the finest gradation *you* in its current developmental state. Now, as I tell you all of this, please make sure to bare in mind that words are completely and utterly inadequate, and fall *just* short of being *totally* useless when describing these things. This telling will in no way make you conscious of the truth of the matter, but it will allow for some semblance of orientation on your part in the world you *now perceive*.

"Along with your sole, you have numerous levels of layers of notions, perceptions, and in general, all manner of various ideas of identity that are superimposed *onto* your 'soul.'

"It's *kind of* like you're an onIon. Generally, when 'souls' arrive here, they are composed of few, if any, layers of their 'onion.' In your case, however, almost all of your layers are intact. Your 'soul' is that which contains that part that perceives the true nature of the place you are *now* in. In your case, however, since you are perceiving all of this through more layers than just about *anyone* else who is here, as a result of having so many layers superimposed upon your 'soul,' your most essential element, that is that which is developing *within* your soul, views this place through a variety of 'filters' that *prevent it,* from perceiving the truth that's surrounding **YU**."

As the driver uttered these final words he motioned for Tim to **stop**. Tim found himself absorbed and perplexed by all that the driver had said, and felt quite dizzy. Through his dizziness, however, he did stop at the driver's behest, and, looking **around** *him*, coming out of *his* daze of thoughts for a moment, he saw that he stood precisely on a division between the field he and the driver had just a moment ago been walking upon, and a massive expanse of sand that started under the front half of his foot and stretched out far before him. Tim saw a great *DESERT*.

Looking out ahead into this abrupt change of scenery, Tim saw several cacti dotting the wide span of sand. He saw wandering the sand *very large* scorpions and a variety of snakes freely roaming the great expanse. Seeing the snakes and scorpions made him feel a bit nervous as a waft of warm air rose up and struck in front of him at his *face*. Despite the ominous imagery spread before him, and the winds slapping at his facade, he calmed himself by remembering that he apparently, at the moment, had no body that could die. Unfortunately, his self-assurances didn't ease his tensions quite to the extent he had hoped.

Much like in the feeled, there were many people sitting in **meditation in the desert.** He could swear that several of the people meditating looked exactly like some of those he saw in the field.

He noticed no rocks in the immediate vicinity, and he noticed that the sand under the front part of his feet, the part of his feet that was in the desert side, felt remarkably soft. In the distance he saw that the speck they had been walking in the direction of was now quite a bit closer, something of a larger speck with a much more definable shape, but that it was still far off. He had a strong suspicion that he was going to be walking through the desert much sooner than later to get to that large spot in the distance.

"What you see before you," began the driver, "is the *second* manifestation of Heaven. By now I have a strong suspicion that you have noticed people meditating in *that*, the second manifestation of Heaven, much as they were in the first? Perhaps you have also noticed those meditating on the division line upon which we currently stand between manifestations?"

Tim looked again into the desert before him, then down the division line to the right and to the left, looked at the driver, and nodded in the affirmative. He considered for a moment that they were, indeed, still standing on the division line between "manifestations."

"The rare few, as before," continued the driver, "are meditating from the 'earthly plane.' The rest, as before, are attempting to meditate into further manifestations, most failing miserably, and trying to realize greater universal truth. Then, there are those whom you see meditating directly **on _THE_ line**."

Tim looked down the line again to his right and to his left. **Right** by his feet, to the **right** of *his* feet, sitting in *full* lotus position, was *a **man*** meditating on **_THE_** line between manifestations.

"Those sitting between manifestations are *rarely* meditators that I affectionately call 'truly lost,' but rather mostly meditators raising their consciousness into the next manifestation, *or* coming out of the next manifestation."

Tim looked down again, and, sure enough, the gentleman he had seen meditating to his right a moment ago was gone.

"So, Tim, have you ever meditated before?" asked the driver.

Tim shook his head no.

"Sit upon the line, cross your legs, close your eyes, and *try* to relax," directed the driver.

Tim did as he was told.

"Now, try to understand, boy, that you will be sort of 'reshaping' the workings of your 'makeup,' and, as is such, your perceptions will be altered accordingly."

Tim had an awkward, uncertain feeling growing inside him as he **_listened_** to the **_driver SPEAK_**.

"Essentially, since you don't have a body to inhibit you *at the moment*, you'll pretty naturally fall into a 'deep meditative trance,' type of state, and as this happens, you may find your most essential self is temporarily *freed* from the rest of your 'filters,' and, as is such, you will most likely start to *feel* some level of separation anxiety as the most real 'you' begins to dissociate from what you generally **think** is . . . 'you.' Again, I can't really sum it up with words. Just know that you might start feeling kind of weird, and that that's natural, and you have nothing to fear since 'you' *will* come back. **Now**, **see** if you cannot relax . . ."

The driver's voice began to **_trail-on_** as Tim did his best to relax himself. It took Tim a minute or **two** to *really* get **_comfortable_** site-ting.

Initially, Tim experienced light coming through his eyelids, but *his* focus, and all *he* could find to think about just then, was the odd notions encouraged by the driver that this wasn't *really* light coming through what weren't *really* **his** eyelids. He sat thinking like this, perfectly still, for what seemed to *him* like the passing of ten or fifteen minutes. He began feeling very restive, and *very* uncomfortable in his form and thoughts, when his mind suddenly stated through the unrest of *his* mind, "They aren't really *your* thoughts either," and finally was able to let **_his-self GO_** in Entirety, Feeling **_NOW_** as **_ONE_** with the **_LIGHT_** that surrounded *him*.

Tim dwelt in *this **LIGHT*** for some time, and as he **_DID_**, he began to feel blades of grass poking into him from behind and supporting a "form," which he now **only tentatively** recognized as **_BEING_** *his*. He then **_FELT_** as though his form was melting into the grass . . . or was it that he was feeling the grass melt into him? And then he remembered that what he thought he was, he wasn't. And then he **became** the grass, and it was only den that he noticed the sand *under his feet* and a percentage of his legs. And then, as though it were *the* most natural thing to do, he started to melt into, or rather *become*, the sand. And then knew only his form, but his form was now only sand and grass and light, and then, things **began** to become strange.

Tim briefly flashed on his entire life as though remembering it all at once, and yet specifically in chronological order. His childhood, his father, his mother, a twenty-car collision on the freeway caused by a bus his father had been on, women, women, women, school, a job that he by no means loved but could live with, women, and a bus with a driver that looked exactly like his father. Tim's life entered and left his consciousness, and he saw the present, *only* the present. He saw a form, "his" form sitting in meditation, but he no longer *knew* himself. He merely felt that he was afraid with nothing to fear, and that he could move forward without knowing how, or why, or where. And he experienced this "Heaven" move away from him as he grew closer to *it*, and he felt a consciousness, *his* consciousness, moving deeper and deeper into this queer concept "Heaven."

Tim saw the sands pass before him. He saw meditators sitting in meditation. Some of these in meditation he *became*, and he knew them as they knew him, and he knew that **they are** by knowing **him**, and he **_NEW_** that in other circumstances and in a more "corporeal" manner, they would probably, maybe, meet. He saw the length of the second manifestation, and it suddenly turned dark, and consciousness began to be perceived as though in flashes out of the darkness.

He saw a wall moving as though alive. He saw closer, and many worms wiggling and wriggling in a wall of mud three inches thick. Long earthworms made the wall alive. Then he saw a hand, and a mouth, and he then didn't want to see more, and "he" *moved* **on**. He flashed on angry, bloodshot eyes. Then he flashed on all manner of insidious-looking devices of torture, but he knew that they weren't for *him* __*NOW*__, and he felt that somehow they were *kindly*, though why he felt this, he did not know. The image of these devices faded out as he heard an un-godly, in-*human* scream pierce through him, and saw in the darkness a trickle of blood that reflected a part of his own body's face. This image finished, fading, and he saw an orb of **PURE** gold, and no-thing *else*. He saw __*THE*__ orb, and was drawn closer and closer to __*IT*__ when, suddenly, all turned __*PERFECT*__ly black. Then, Tim knew a *peace* he had __*ALLWAYS*__ known before, and, in *effect,* experienced what could **only** be described as a "true nothingness." *He* did not exist. No-thing did. Just – . . . And he knew he could-not stay *there*, that it wasn't his "time," not for *him*, *yet* . . . And *he* flung himself away and came back to where "the form," *his* form, sat. And Tim opened *his* eyes, and could *see*.

Never **before** had Tim seen as he did __*NOW*__, and as *he* saw, *he* sat and felt tears stream down *his* face, though he knew not *quite* why, except that he was filled with a joy he had never had before at the realization that he had eyes to **see** the **light** that **surrounded** *him*. Light, which he had never *seen* be-4.

Tim took *the* hand that was held out before *him* and a*rose*. Side-by-side Tim stood with the driver. Hands still held, they stepped forward, and the driver spoke. "Welcome to the second manifestation of Heaven." And further into the desert they walked.

Book 4
Manifestation 2: Just Deserts

Snakes; long, dusty, and wielding formidable rattles and fangs slithered freely and often between Tim's bare feet as he and the driver walked through the desert. Snakes weren't the only things walking this expanse of dryness either. Large, furry tarantulas of black, bright oranges, and beige, as well as huge scorpions with ominous tails, were as frequent company as the snakes, though they tended not to be as inclined to accompany and become acquainted with him as the snakes were. As he made his journey through the sands, however, every so often a tarantula would find its way across his foot, or a scorpion would crawl out from under a large rock and walk with the journeyers a ways.

Before his meditation, upon seeing these apparently poisonous entities traversing the desert floor, he had been more than a bit frightened of these comparatively small creatures, unable to shake the notion that they might somehow do him harm. A very short time after his experience with meditation, however, not only did he not fear these critters scampering across the expanse of desert, but he felt instead an incredible sense of calmness within him that these creatures barely disturbed in the least. In fact, after just a short time walking and noting that none of these animals were making it a point to do him any harm whatsoever, not only did the most infinitesimal traces of fear leave him completely, but he even began to appreciate the diversity the creatures brought to the landscape, and almost, *almost* enjoyed feeling the differing textures pass by his ankles from time to time. Instead of recoiling in dread while thinking about the various forms of venom these creatures possessed that might do a great harm to what he had previously been certain was *his* body, he now not only felt that he had nothing to fear from these small, intricate beings, but even found himself absorbed in the watching of the great minutiae and detail of their forms as well as the gentle rockings and swayings and subtle, graceful movements with which they propelled themselves over the sands.

Occasionally, while they walked, Tim found himself stopping to look deeply at the leg of a tarantula that happened to be walking by. Or he would stop to ponder the nuances of the device that was the scorpion's tail. He would feel the pattern on a large rattlesnake that passed by his heel and examine the intricate geometries of the beings that he previously would never have thought in a million years to get close enough to examine.

Meanwhile, he saw people in the desert in a state of play much as in the fields, but with far less frequency. It seemed as though many people loved the desert environment and felt safe to play in it in a way they never would have on Earth. Unlike in the field, people were inclined to play *with* the animals. He saw people throwing around tarantulas like baseballs, scorpions like frisbees, and jumping rope with rattlesnakes. But for the most part, they were simply walking in the same direction that he and the driver were. There were still folks occasionally doing a handstand or running around the sands, tossing sand at each other and jumping very high and catching each other in midair and then falling back to the ground while laughing, still people eating sand, which he declined to try despite his mild curiosity spurred by watching some shovel fistfuls of the stuff into their mouths. But compared to the last manifestation, all of this activity was fairly subdued. For the most part he noticed much less lovemaking and much more walking.

Much like in the first manifestation, he also noticed a number of people sitting in meditation, though there were apparently not as many as there had been in the first manifestation. He found himself chuckling lightly as he recalled *being* some of those sitting cross-legged that he walked by. A few of those meditating whom he passed set off a very deep feeling of déjà vu in him, which he thought was odd since he could swear he recognized them despite the fact that he didn't specifically recall them from either his meditation or any other of his previous experiences, either on Earth or in Heaven.

As he perceived these people and had his feelings of déjà vu, he flashed on hints of emotion contrary to those he felt when seeing the creatures of the desert. Tim, being suddenly unsure about his memory and why he might remember something that he felt that he should have no reason to remember, for a brief moment became once again unsure of *himself*. As he felt this sudden uncertainty about the nature of what he had a moment ago been pretty sure was him, his feelings gave rise to the slightest wisp of fear that ran down along two or three hairs on the back of his neck. He found this slight discomfort easy to brush away as he continued walking through the desert, but it was minor moments such as these that began slowly to chip away at his bliss as he continued on his journey.

Walking ever onward toward the continuously growing speck ahead of them, he began noticing that the people around them who were walking, whom he previously supposed had been moving in the same direction that he and the driver were, were actually *heading* a bit to the right of the direction he and the driver were currently pointed toward. As they walked further and grew closer to their apparent destination, he saw that what looked to be a mile or two to the right of where the bus sat, there was what appeared to be a large hill. A little to the left of that hill was what appeared from a distance to be a fuzzy, or rather hazy, box that seemed to have a very long line of people standing in front of it. He also started noticing that some of those walking in the direction of the line, if not the hill itself, seemed to be walking right out of thin air and then heading toward the left, toward the back of the line. He wasn't accustomed to seeing people walking out of thin air, and thinking this to be a bit strange, looked up at the driver. Before he had managed to utter a single word, the driver answered just as though he had heard Tim's thoughts aloud. What was truly queer in this instance, however, was that not only did he not ask his question to the driver, but that as the driver responded, his lips did not move, his gaze stayed fixed and focused straight ahead, and never once did the driver look at him or in any other way move any of the features above his neck.

"They," "spoke" the driver, "are those, just like the others you've seen, trying to find their way into higher manifestations of Heaven. They are highly pragmatic in their approach to achieve higher 'levels' of Heaven, but what works well in this manifestation, they'll likely discover, generally isn't nearly as practical in further manifestations.

"You already know that what you see, in this place at least, isn't always what you get. Well, there is of course, like with all things, a reason why you perceive these 'souls' *appearing* out of 'thin air.' When they come to the first manifestation they lose all connection with their old . . . 'forms.' Once these souls begin to get . . . 'oriented,' however, often they begin to, and have a longing to, remember their old lives and their past. As a result, these souls begin to cling onto any 'echo' of their old selves that still remains with them. From these echoes form coarser layers around their purer state of 'soul,' and as a result these souls become more like you, imbued with an outward 'shell' of sorts that allows them to feel safer, and which at the same time allows them to perceive this highly abstract place in 'filtered,' more 'graspable,' 'earthly' terms. Some of these souls cling so strongly to their echoes that we have to reincarnate them on the spot. Having altogether lost any semblance of a notion of reality, by being sent back, hopefully they will be better suited for a continuation of evolution through the various manifestations once they have experienced life from a completely new and different perspective. While reincarnation for *this specific reason* rarely happens, it is interesting to note that Hindus tend to have a substantially lower rate of reincarnation than just about any other culture or society on Earth.

"What you are perceiving as people suddenly appearing are beings who wish to pass through the manifestations as quickly as possible, already having a sense of the true nature of the place, and who aren't as attached to their residual echoes of what they used to be, their perceptions of self, as those in the first manifestation. These coming to the second manifestation directly still perceive the cow, but only briefly and as they make their way as far through Heaven as they can before their individuated level of false-identification catches up to them." After the driver had finished his "statement," Tim was speechless and more than a little confused, and they walked onward in silence.

———————

Tim and the driver were quite close to the bus now. Tim considered the reality of having feet in quotation marks as he pondered their apparent struggle with "their" perceived reality; suffice to say the consistency of the "sand" had changed dramatically since they had first begun walking through the desert. Initially, upon entering the desert, the sand had been as a fine-grained powder that was extremely pleasant to walk on, much like walking on a ground made of baking flour. As Tim walked further through the desert, however, the ground gradually had become rougher and a bit tougher. About midway to the bus, the ground had been as typical beach sand on the California coast, maybe a little coarser and with a couple more pebbles thrown in, but otherwise highly comparable. The sand was *now* beginning to become fairly rocky in texture, which was far less than comfortable to Tim's feet, which at this point in time were beginning to feel like two cuts of ill-tenderized meat, especially in conjunction with the rocks that were starting to stick into them with every other step.

Tim was also very aware of the presence of "heat." He was reluctant to actually call it heat, since it wasn't exactly like experiencing hot weather on the surface of the Earth. The only words that he found to describe the feeling that gradually grew on him as he walked further into the desert, however, were, "It's hot!" It felt as though the "light," which radiated in some subtle way from *everything*, and continuously from the "sky," was gaining in intensity with every step he took onward toward the bus. Step by step through this omnipresent radiance, at this point in his journey through the desert, the heat was becoming a "highly noticeable factor" in his continuing desert trek.

———————

Finally, the light being both comforting as well as almost completely unbearably scorching in a suffocating kind of way, coupled with the minor boulders he now walked on, a far cry from the powder-esque sands upon which he had originally tread when entering the desert, Tim and the driver had come at last to the bus. The door of the bus folded open and to its side as he and the driver arrived at it, as though it knew instinctively that its driver and passenger had returned. He had another momentary lapse of disquiet as the bus opened itself, but at this point he trusted the bus much more than the ground on which he presently walked and was more than a little relieved to take his feet off whatever jagged stones they were pressing against as he followed the driver up and into the bus. He also found gratitude to be no longer perpetually pelted by the Heavenly light which now seemed to be radiating, thankfully, outside the bus. The driver took his seat and Tim found himself actually *happy* to be on the bus, reclaiming his "old" seat next to one of the impenetrable windows on the right of the bus, the vehicle that promised to bring him ever closer to his impending doom.

He noted the driver shift ever so slightly, and the bus came to life, slowly, starting to roll along again.

Having been previously fixated on getting his feet off the rocks and onto the bus, he hadn't noticed, but looking out of the front window now, he saw clearly a very long line of "people." This line extended out, apparently from the foot of what appeared to be a fairly small hill, the same one he could remember noticing before. This long line of people went back as far as his eyes could see and ended at what seemed to be something around a couple of miles away from where the bus currently sat, several hundred yards away from the front of the hill.

As the bus rolled on, slowly, next to the line of people, he saw the box he had remembered seeing before, far less fuzzy and hazy now. He noticed as the bus got closer that the people seemed not to be standing in front of the hill exactly, but apparently in front of the box. The box itself seemed to be a simple cube-shaped structure with windows on each side.

The bus continued to roll slowly beside the line of people over the rocks that the sand had become. He mused to himself that it wasn't nearly as unusual as it once might have been to experience the smoothness and silence with which the bus rode over the myriad large rocks under its wheels.

The bus continued rolling beside the line fairly slowly, and Tim was more than a little impressed to see this, probably the longest line he had ever seen in his life, without a doubt comprised of no fewer than hundreds of thousands of people. About five people or so from the front of the line, the bus stopped.

He saw quite clearly now that at the front of the line was a booth. The booth stood 25 yards or so from the big, black, gaping hole, which apparently led into the hill that sat tranquilly before them. Coming off the booth, on either side, was an arm which indicated that this was apparently a tollbooth. On one side of the booth, behind the arm, was the line of people. On the other side, behind the other arm, was the bus.

On the bus side of the tollbooth was a sort of silver bucket. Tim saw that on the other side of the booth there were a couple of holes cut into the window, apparently so that people could converse between the glass and exchange *something*, he didn't imagine they could possibly be using money in Heaven, under the glass. It struck him as odd that *any* kind of exchange of material goods would be required to be made in a place that seemed to him to be the epitome of incorporeality. He also noticed a sign in the window on the "people side," but he was unable to read the sign from his position on the bus.

They sat for a short length of time, perhaps five minutes or so, behind the arm of the tollbooth. Tim was about to ask why they were waiting when the driver suddenly extended his arm and pointed his finger in the direction of where they had been walking several minutes ago, or rather from the direction the people had been walking. He looked through the window in the direction the driver pointed.

Out of nowhere Tim saw a man materialize, and walk toward the tollbooth. A minute later he was at the side of the booth reading the sign in the window. The man looked at the people waiting in line. He looked the line over, up and down a couple of times, then looked at the sign, then looked at the black opening in the hill to his right. He looked back at the sign, back at the people, back at the hole, and stroked his chin. Tim noticed hairs beginning to sprout out of his chin as the man stroked it. The man looked again toward the people, then turned toward the hill and began walking. The man sidestepped the arm of the booth and, within seconds, was disappearing into the blackness, the only sight that could be seen in the opening of the hill.

Initially, as the man had been surveying the scene, nothing "out of the ordinary" took place. When the man started heading for the hill, however, and especially when he sidestepped the arm of the booth, pandemonium broke out in the line he left behind him. Those in line started shouting at the man, yelling for him to take his place at the back of the line where he "belonged," and so on. When the man's form had finally faded out of view, people continued shouting, yelling up to the very tops of their lungs in anger.

Some started to try to leave the line so as to follow the man who had entered the cave, but they were quickly pulled back into the line and scolded by the others waiting, and in some cases, even punched, slapped, or kicked for trying to do as the other man had done. A small handful of people, sixteen or so, actually made it safely to the opening leading into the hill, and thankfully, disappeared without incurring the wrath of the rest of the line aside from the handful of threats and curses that followed them into the hill.

After these individuals had dissolved into the blackness and beyond Tim's sight, he heard what sounded like a voice, almost like an echo, saying, "Knock, knock," from somewhere deep inside the cave.

Finally, the commotion began to die down. When it had finally and completely ceased, no less than a thousand "people" disappeared from the line. As these "people" vanished, the rest in the line moved up quietly and calmly. Tim also noticed more people coming up to the booth from the direction of the field and reading the sign, but all of these people began walking to the back of the line after reading the sign. In fact, that one man who had first entered into the hillside was the only person he saw entering the hill solitarily after reading the sign. The other handful he had seen go in hadn't stopped to read the sign, though they had presumably read it before they had originally taken their places in the line.

Tim turned toward the driver, and before he had a chance to ask the questions coming to his mind, the driver spoke aloud.

"They were reincarnated. That is, those who disappeared from the line. These being's souls are far too coarse and underdeveloped to pass any further, and now, those of a more quarrelsome nature must return to the earthly realm to work on the composition of the contents of their souls further.

"Now, the one who entered, they called him Walter when he was with body, is very gifted. He'll make it at least to the fourth manifestation with no difficulty and little pause. You can always tell the truly gifted, they never move on without taking a few with them. Those others you saw leave have notable ability too, and have found their way to the third manifestation with comparative ease. Good fortune combined with good inner composition of soul! Yes, they may make it even to the fifth with but a little perseverance.

"Walter himself seems to be seven-bound in a hurry. Maybe they'll even make it further within the next several centuries, God only knows. It is always good to see progression in the synthesis and growth of the inward composition of souls. You see a soul from creation, and just several tiny millennia later . . .

"Ah! But I am sentimental. And, if I'm not mistaken, you still want to know what the sign says, don't you?" Tim caught the driver's gaze in the rearview mirror and nodded in the affirmative.

"The sign," began the driver, "says simply, 'Will Return Shortly.' You would be amazed how many centuries, if not millennia, if not googolplexes of eons, people will wait in that line before they even *begin* to contemplate moving, and even then, not as many progress to the third manifestation as you might think. While certain forces may work in mysterious ways, generally, people do not, and we always see the ones who *do* coming from a mile away."

The driver smiled as he said this and pulled a lever by his side, apparently shifting gear. "I think we've spent more than enough time in this desert, and there probably won't be much to see in this group, aside from growth of course, for another 50 to 100 years, if not longer."

With that said, the bus slowly pulled up to the arm of the booth and the driver rolled down his window. The driver reached into a pocket of his pants, and Tim swore he saw that the driver had retracted, between his thumb and forefinger, a small ball of pure light, which, though bright, did no harm to his eyes. He immediately flashed on the memory of a very dark tunnel, which he felt that he had been in lifetimes ago. He blinked, and instead of a ball of light, the driver now seemed to be holding a shiny, silver coin between his thumb and forefinger. The driver reached the arm that held the coin out the rolled-down window, and, with a grunt, threw upward. Fourteen seconds or so went by before Tim saw a streaking flash fall fast into the silver bucket attached to the side of the tollbooth. The arm of the booth lifted, and the driver spoke. "Of course lad, those with more immediate means need not wait while others will wait to walk ways cleared by those with will and without a single thought in mind of who waits behind them to walk without will, aside from the will to walk."

With that said, the bus rolled smoothly into the darkness of the opening leading into the hill.

As the bus entered the now familiar deep darkness of pitch-black, Tim noticed that he didn't mind being surrounded by the total absence of light this second time going into it. He actually found it soothing to be in this variation on void. He did hope, however, not to have to take another *walk* in the darkness toward unknown ends.

The bus stayed at a steady pace for enough time to relax a good while or so before the darkness gradually began to lighten. Suddenly Tim could make out the dim light of a torch in the far distance. The driver turned to him, looked him directly in the eyes, and with a grin on his face said, "Welcome to the third manifestation of Heaven!"

Book 5
Manifestation 3: Tola'El

Shortly after the driver welcomed Tim to the third manifestation of Heaven, the bus reached the torch. The torch illuminated a bend in the path and the bus turned to reveal what looked to be another torch vaguely visible in the distance. Once the bus arrived at the next torch, a bend in the path brought it face to face with another distant torch. This process continued on in the same manner for no less than an hour: a torch, a bend, another torch in the distance, and so on.

While traveling, apparently, deeper and deeper into the cave, Tim had time to reflect at length on the path he now found himself traveling down. He felt as though his travels had already been very long. The monotony he was now experiencing he found to be a relieving and relaxing change of pace. The subtle light of the torches was comforting after having spent so much of his journey in total darkness. He found himself contemplating the duality of the simplicity and yet incredible miracle that was the torches' fire.

As these thoughts went through his mind about the nature of the subtle illuminations lightening what he would otherwise perceive as darkness, he noticed that, though not by much, the light coming from the next turn down the road seemed to be slightly brighter than the light had been from previous turns.

As the bus made that next turn, he saw the cause of heightened illumination, and he saw that this section of the tunnel was particularly long. At the end of this long, straight section of tunnel, he saw two large pillars supporting an archway. In front of each pillar stood a tall torch with fairly tall flames casting light upon both the archway and the ground. At the top of the pillars, at the base of the arch-proper, on either side was the head of a snake biting the tail of the snake whose head rested on the other pillar. From one fanged mouth of stone a slithery body would arch upward until it reached the top of the arch, where sat a large, three-pointed symbol. The symbol was a triangle with the tip of each point etched further into the stone, so that each tip was also a triangle. Behind the symbol the snakes' bodies disappeared, only to reemerge on the other side of the triangle where, after having arched itself a little higher, the body would finally descend into a tail that found its way into the other snake's mouth. In this way each snake sort of acted as half of what looked to be a figure eight turned on its side, with a triangle intersecting the place the snakes' bodies crossed.

Seeing the archway, Tim, though still relatively at ease, couldn't help but feel some rise of apprehension about what he may see once on the other side of that archway.

Luminated by the light of the two torches before the columns, he noticed the path they were traveling on. The path was divided into what appeared to be three different substances. The very center of the path was apparently a stream, somehow simultaneously placid and flowing. This center of the path was wide enough for one person to comfortably walk down had it been made of concrete, though how deep the water was he did not know. On either side of this middle path of water was a path that seemed to be paved in gold. Looking at the width of these paths of twin strips of golden substance, it seemed that either side was as wide as the middle path, and four inches or so higher than the top of the stream. By Tim's estimation the bus must be rolling on the golden paths, a wheel on either path. Beside the golden paths, on either side, he perceived a row of cloud filling the space between the golden path and the wall of the cave. In height the clouds rose no higher than the windows of the bus, perhaps five feet or so above the golden road.

Slowly, the bus continued moving forward. As the bus gradually moved closer to the archway, the light of the torches grew, shedding more light by the second. He noticed that he felt quite clearly that the rays of light emitting from the torches cast a sort of heat upon his cheeks.

Not sure what wonders could possibly be reveled after this fairly awe-inspiring archway, and being curious, he felt the need to ask the driver a question. "Are we already at the fourth—"

"Nope!" The driver cut him off before he had a chance to finish. "An eighth the struggle of the previous manifestations, and already you would be through to another? Perhaps I should have welcomed you here once through the greater entrance up ahead, but then I would have been telling less than a half-truth. No, my boy, you're closer to the end of this manifestation than I may let on, in a sense, but dear child, in a much truer sense, you have not even begun to perceive what this little slice of Heaven has to reveal."

Tim had another question. "Well, why has the path suddenly become—"

"It's been that way for a while." The driver cut him off again before he had the opportunity to finish uttering his inquiry. "You simply hadn't noticed before the path on which you, well, tread. This road on which we ride through Heaven is threefold, a different substance for differing forms of beings.

"You see, if any soul has made it this far into Heaven, they must have developed in truth and perfected the state of their truest substance to such a degree that they have, as it is said, that necessary to walk on water. Of course take note, this is *not* Earth, and there is more of, what you would call, metaphor here for the sake of your perception representative of the true method of conveyance used by progressing souls, than the truth of the way these beings continue on *their* journeys. But, suffice to say, without belief that a road may lead to a place that one wishes to go, a person will never willingly set foot on that path to begin with. And without faith, that same person will never arrive at the destination they seek."

As the driver paused for a moment in his explanation, Tim saw that they had covered a bit more than half the distance to the archway than there had been when he had first looked down the long stretch of road. He noticed that the light from the torches was much brighter now than when they had first entered this section of the cave. He felt his cheeks were warmed almost to the point of discomfort by the rays of emanating light more acutely than he had before from the torches ahead.

"The golden road," continued the driver, "is used by beings higher than the souls finding their way through Heaven. That is to say, this road is used by beings that are of such substance that they frequent an environment such as this the way a human would frequent the various highways of earth. Here I suppose *I* would be a satisfactory example for the type of being inclined to travel upon *this* road. As *I am* ordained to drive what you perceive as *this bus*, this road has been laid so as to allow my vehicle a smooth and direct path for my-self, and those that share something in common with me. How fortunate *you* are, then, to ride upon the golden road; though perhaps not too fortunate, as you anticipate where this path will inevitably lead *you*." As the driver uttered the final word of this sentiment, Tim could feel a wide smirk form across the driver's lips without the driver having to turn his head toward Tim an inch. He also felt the discomfort of the heat on his cheeks slowly begin to spread to the rest of his face.

The driver continued. "As far as the final section of this road upon which we travel is concerned . . . well, let's just say that as water is laid for those more like you to walk upon, and gold laid for the vehicles of those more like me, whatever name you would use for that which is conveyed upon the clouds, by whatever respective vehicle the likes of which you could not begin to begin to conceive, is that which is, and GOD *willing always* shall. AMEN!"

With this concluding remark the bus was very close to the archway. This close, the detail of the snakes, their scales, seemed incredibly real but for the color of the stone in which they were carved. As the bus began to pass under the archway, the window Tim sat next to passed as close to the right-side torch as possible, and as the bus passed by the torches, he felt the heat of the fire strike his face directly from both sides; from both torches. The heat that lashed out at his face in this moment was at least very uncomfortable, and in truth, much closer to practically unbearable. The brightness that entered his periphery with the sudden swell of heat was blinding, and for the first time in a comparative while, he felt incredible discomfort.

The bus continued under the arch and he found himself relaxing ever so much, momentarily, the further away he felt himself pulled from the searing source of illumination he had recently experienced into his now-considered friend, the darkness.

His lull into soothing darkness was not too long, however, for as the bus cleared the archway he was completely overcome by a white light. So much light came suddenly flooding into his vision that he found himself blinded. Though the light was much brighter than when passing by the flames, he felt no heat this time, but a certain kind of coolness instead. The coolness he perceived seemed to permeate the air around him; he perceived that it manifested almost as a sort of dankness. Despite his best efforts to discern the world around him, however, his eyes could not help him perceive the reality of his situation.

Tim felt the bus stop. Though he perceived light of some form, his eyes could not make out outward appearance.

He heard the door of the bus open, and the driver speak very simply, "Come with me."

He stood and felt his way the best he could toward where he had heard the driver's voice. The driver said gently, "Give me your hand." He reached out, instinctively putting his hand into the warm grip of the driver's.

Slowly, he and the driver walked down the steps of the bus. The driver warned, "Be careful of this last step," as Tim's right foot began its decent down to the ground below.

His foot touched the ground with something of a squish to his ear and a feel of thick spaghetti to his bare foot. He heard something like muttering nearby, and the unmistakable sound of slurping, mooshing, and smacking of lips. He marveled at all he was able to perceive and wasn't half sure just how badly he wanted to regain his sight.

Guided by the driver, his feet had now made the harrowing trek off the bus, and as they did, the driver pulled on his arm, indicating that he should begin walking forward. As he walked forward he noticed through his blindness that under the "spaghetti," the ground was incredibly smooth. After taking a few more steps forward, he noticed that the ground beneath his feet felt grainy and that he felt a cool, soothing dampness brush across his cheeks and over his nose as he walked on.

A few steps later the cool crispness that had caressed his face ceased, and where a moment ago the air was refreshingly damp, the air had now become comparatively thick and dank. The ground under the slimy mass surrounding his ankles was very stony, and the air hung with a humid, wet, warm staleness that was less than inviting. He was more content now than ever, being more reliant on his other senses rather than experiencing an instantaneous revelation of the causes effecting his nose by way of his eyes, though he wasn't wholly displeased when singular light-like illuminations were ever so slowly starting to come into focus around him.

Several more steps later, he noticed that the consistency of the ground underfoot was becoming finer and finer. The feel of smooth stones became the feel of smooth gravel, and the feel of gravel turned more and more into what seemed to be a ground made of mud. He also felt that the further he walked, the deeper the spaghetti he walked in was becoming. The spaghetti was slowly rising up his lower shins the further he went. He could now make out the distinct forms of the fire of torches several yards away. He also saw what looked like a large form moving into itself, yet not roaming. It was stationary, but animated. As he grew closer to the forms in front of him, the feeling underfoot of gravel mixed with mud turned into a feeling of sand mixed with mud, and felt even muddier as he went on.

As the two moved closer to the shape slowly pulsing and moving with strange rhythms in front of him, his vision also began to begin its return. No more than fifteen paces away, he began to make out what looked like people at a table, all but one sitting. The one who stood apparently went to and from the table with what seemed like a very long spoon, serving those who sat and waited. Though the picture was slowly forming and coming into focus, he still wasn't quite able to see.

The one serving seemed to be going to the back wall, rubbing the spoon against the wall, and then dropping the contents of the spoon into bowls set out in front of those sitting in wait. Things more focused now than ever, the contents of the spoon seemed to be very thick spaghetti. Tim noticed for the first time a circular light of sorts glowing over the heads of those sitting at the table. It was a rather beautiful scene, seen through a slight haze, all of these glowing rings above what looked like tens of thousands of people all sitting at the same extraordinarily long table. As Tim slooshed through the material in which he walked, now a quarter or so up his legs, he noticed that which he was walking through seemed almost to be pushing back on him as he walked.

The forms were all clear, though the details were still not quite ready to be fully discerned. Tim stood only a few steps behind one of those sitting at the table when he took his final step forward. The ground was still quite squarmy and slimy, slushing around his legs and now nearing halfway up his shins. His feet felt mud squish between his toes, and the "spaghetti" around his legs almost felt as though it had a motion of its own. And then . . .

Eyes open, mind now fully aware, details suddenly focused, Tim jumped back three feet with a scream pitched of horror emanating from his throat. Finishing his first deafening screech of terror upon completing his decent, his throat found itself unable to hold back a second the second he landed. He stood amidst a sea of earthworms squirming around his lower legs, and the terror his voice let out like a siren refused to relent.

Around him, surrounding him, everywhere he looked, worms on top of worms crawling under worms, around worms and through worms. He had been walking through them since his first step off the bus. Now that he had regained his vision and had realized what he had been walking through, seeing what things now *seemed* to be left him in a state so far removed from mere panic that his body became utterly rigid. His voice worked fully automatically as though a fire siren, and his consciousness was desperate to leave this apparent physical form which chained it so steadfastly to the environment in which he unfortunately found himself suddenly enfolded and entirely entrapped. Had he been in more earthly a place, in fact, Tim's consciousness almost certainly would have escaped deeply into his mind and left him with an indefinite case of catatonia. Here, however, it seemed that his state of being was a far cry from what it would have been on Earth; though the loudness of Tim's voice was certainly testing the limits of just how far away he would have to be for his cry *not* to be heard on Earth.

The veritable sea of worms Tim found himself wading through was certainly a shock, but that was merely a slice of the perceptions sending waves of terror throughout his being. In front of him there were many people sitting at a *very* long table. In front of each person, on the table, sat a bowl. On the half of the table to Tim's left, most of the bowls in front of the people seemed to be empty. On the half of the table to Tim's right, the majority of the bowls in front of the people appeared to be full, brimming over with worms.

A figure in a black-hooded cloak passing back and forth before the table held a long, deep wooden spoon filled with worms. The figure was dumping worms into the empty bowls, and when it had emptied the contents of its spoon, it reached the spoon back behind the table and rubbed the spoon against the backmost wall of the cave.

The wall of the cave was as though composed of mud and looked alive with worms crawling over it, through it, and in it. For hundreds of feet in either direction, this wall was covered in mud and crawling with worms whose skin reflected soft colors reflected by the flames of the torches sticking out through the worms. Freestanding metal-based torches also poked occasionally from out of the ocean of worms. The fire from these torches illuminated on the back wall blood-red worms, pink worms, worms the color of fresh, bright green apples, purple worms and worms of electric blue, dark, but almost having a subtle glow of their own. The worms changed hue and reflected almost metallically in the light of the flames. All of these colors, soft and unusual, made the back wall of the cave alive with these multi-colored dwellers of the earth that had so startled him. Spanning the wall as far as he could see in either direction, he could swear he saw spread out diagonally from ceiling to floor, top left to bottom right, the faint outline of a worm a thousand times his own size breathing, faintly squirming; the worms crawling over that section of the cave rising and falling ever so gently.

Of all these sights to be seen, however, the people sitting at the table, eating, made up the vast majority of what Tim's screaming was really about. At first glance the bright rings of light floating playfully around the heads of those sitting at the table almost began to slightly ease the tremendous shock that pierced through Tim as all these sights and perceptions suddenly flooded into his field of vision. The sight of these luminous rings *almost* comforted Tim, but then, Tim perceived the state of these people encircled by their halos, and his real terror began.

Seeing the multi-colored worms in the bowls before the people sitting at the table was disgusting enough. Looking down from the halos and seeing the figure of a man scooping those things into his mouth, however, was another matter entirely. Tim wished he could vomit or pass out or anything to release his mind through an action of his body. But he couldn't make his body do anything. His body was as though on autopilot, and freezing up and screaming seemed all that it was willing to do at the moment. So, he watched as those at the table scooped the slimy, red and pink and purple and blue and green worms into their mouths.

Some cringed, quivered, and shook with utter disgust, and he felt that these reactions were obviously reasonable, though why they would bring the worms to their mouths to begin with was beyond him. Others ate the worms without noticeable emotion at all. Some smiled as they ate, much to his total disbelief, and it was these people who were, to Tim's sight, missing considerable portions of flesh where he was of the unshakeable conviction their stomachs should be.

While in the previous two manifestations of Heaven the beings he perceived had for the most part appeared clothed, not one image of a person sitting at this table had any clothing covering their bodies above the waist. Tim wouldn't have thought much of this at a glance, but seeing the various-sized gaping holes in different stomachs around the table, the lack of clothing on these people's upper bodies struck Tim with a particularly resounding emphasis.

Those showing negative or neutral emotion were apparently left intact, but those who appeared to be happy as they ate, those sitting with wide, pleasant, contented, calm smiles unflinching upon their faces as they thrust spoonful after spoonful of worms into their mouths, were definitely lacking significant portions of their bellies. No intestines or entrails hung out, and it appeared that the various organs that should have been there, to a great extent, were either missing or in some state of being eaten away. In fact, he noticed that as these beings ate, what appeared to be an acid-like substance dripped down and around their exposed organs and bellies further dissolving whatever it touched.

All of these perceptions coalesced the moment his sight returned, and the effect of these perceptions coming together was a sort of terror he had never known to the best of his recollection. Even the Gatekeeper was but a strong second compared to perceptions he was now taking in.

So, there stood Tim amidst this minor sea of gray and pink earthworms, standing stock still as they crawled over his feet, through his toes, and between his legs, screaming at the top of his lungs like no banshee could begin to attempt to duplicate. And it was at this time, after these perceptions had flooded him and he had stood there howling and screeching for the better part of many minutes, that the black-robed figure turned its hooded head toward Tim.

Staring at him now was a face with no skin upon which crawled five, perhaps six worms, some wriggling on the face, some, in part, wriggling *in* the face, blood and pus oozing out where the worms seemed to be stuck in. Tim continued to scream.

———————

After staring at Tim for a couple of minutes, Tim thought this grotesque creature with the long wooden spoon staring at his petrified wailing was finally turning back around to continue feeding the people sitting at the table. While he thought he saw its head turning back toward the table, however, the bloody, pussy mass of muscle crawling with worms that was its face continued staring straight at him while the rest of its head *did* turn around. Then, suddenly, it had three hands, then three arms, two of which held large, long, wooden spoons. Then three feet, then three legs, then two heads. And seamlessly, an exact duplicate was pulling itself out of the original, and before he knew it, a second wormy, skinless face was taking a first step toward him.

Tim continued to stand stock still in terror as his voice tried to hit ever-higher notes. He was incapable of anything else.

As the first fearsome figure returned to the service of those at the table, the second took another step toward him. As that second form took that second step toward him, he thought he could begin to barely perceive an almost imperceptible ray of light emanate out from some point at the top of its oozing, festering forehead.

As it took two more steps, a line of light was clearly beginning to divide its face. Blood, pus, worms, and light were slowly coming toward him step by step. Though on the one hand his horror grew by the footfall, the light, for some reason he as of yet could not discern, almost, *almost,* seemed to soothe him. With each step, the features of this creature's hideous face became ever clearer, but so did the lengthening line of light. As the line grew, ever so slightly, Tim's terror began ever so lightly to let up.

Nine steps toward him, and a line of pure light divided two halves of the mass of festering face filled with wriggling worms. Ten steps, and the two halves of its face began to separate. Eleven steps and the upper third of its face showed of pure light. Twelve steps and the light covered over two thirds of its face, and on the thirteenth step, the creature stopped two steps away from where Tim stood frozen in place. The two flaps that a moment ago had been its face hung for a moment at the side of its head, and then fell, disappearing before they hit the ground. The large, long wooden spoon in its right hand turned into a luminescent staff of a material resembling gold, but translucent as though solid light.

Now, no more than a stride away, Tim gazed into a face composed of a light pure and familiar. Having never seen anything like it before, he did not understand why he felt the sensation of familiarity he did, but it was there nonetheless. For the first time in many minutes his voice desisted its shrill, alarm-esque screal, and his body began to ease ever so slightly.

Tim was soothed by the pure radiance emanating from the face, and heard a sweet voice say almost like a song, "Be still, child." On either side of the being, two luminescent, diaphanous shapes spread outward, and he felt himself so completely enraptured by the being in front of him, and suddenly felt so secure, that not but the faintest memory of worms lingered in his mind.

Tim felt suddenly as though one with the light, and he perceived the essence of words, of thoughts. "Nothing to touch, no harm. You are. It is. Be! . . . Be not! Look at the light, remember, and choose!"

And the pure white that was all around him, encompassing him, enfolding him, engulfing him in its warm radiance, vanished. He stood in a sea of worms, ill at ease but comparably calm; uncomfortable, but not due to a seething terror as just mere moments ago.

Tim felt a hand grip his shoulder. He looked up, and staring at him, over his shoulder, were the big oval eyes of a giant pink bunny. Startled, he jerked and jumped back. A big human hand gripped the chin of the bunny face attached to its human body and pulled the face of the bunny off to reveal the face of a grinning bus driver, who stated reassuringly and with a chuckle, "Sorry kid, didn't mean to spook ya."

With the release of the tension of the last several minutes, Tim let loose a laugh that shook through his body. For that brief moment of laughter he was able to relinquish his anxieties and allow his self to relax entirely.

When Tim stopped laughing and regained some sense of his surroundings, however, he felt at least some amount of discontent at being surrounded by worms and staring at a table filled with all levels of what appeared to be disemboweled people eating worms. Not knowing what else to do, he stared expectantly at the driver. The driver took a step toward him, put his right hand on Tim's left shoulder and pointed with his left hand toward the table. "Looks pretty awful, don't it?"

Tim nodded in the affirmative.

"The beginnings of the liberation of the soul," began the driver. "Now, keep in mind, lad, everything you see is but a poor representation of what the reality of where you are, is. In whatever limited way words will suffice to make some sense out of what you see, however, I will try to explain the general idea of what you think you perceive.

"That," said the driver pointing at the figure in the black hood holding a long, wooden spoon, "is Tola'El, Worm of God. He is what you, in closest approximation, would refer to as an 'Angel.' His job is to feed those who come this far into the Heavenly realm with a manner of divine sustenance created for the purpose of transmuting their 'echo of self-conception' into a form capable of continuing throughout subsequent manifestations of Heaven.

"In this case, the food they consume recreates an element of their self-image if their state of being is in such a state that works in favor of the state the food is trying to create to be created. Take, for example, the round illuminations hovering over and around their heads, what you might refer to as a 'halo.' In order to transmute their sense of being into a state that produces such a "feature," they must already be in a state of being allowing them to take on said further attribute so that they can pass on into future manifestations, such as the one in which we presently dwell.

"In the case of the halo, its purpose is to illuminate the immediate darkness perceived by the soul, so that the soul may be able to progress through the darkness unimpeded and find its way forward. In order to pass beyond the second manifestation, these beings must already possess an inner sense of guidance formed from experiences perceived up to that point that would allow them to step across the threshold between the second and third manifestations of Heaven. Once that step is taken, the halo forms itself as an outer illumination from what it was previously as a form of inner guidance. In this way, the various layers of one's residual echoes of self-perceived being are transmuted in the course of the duration of their passing through the various manifestations of Heaven, until only the truest and most developed result of their journey remains. And at that point . . .

"Now look." The driver pointed toward the table. "In this case, by perceiving themselves as having something reminiscent of a stomach, they cannot pass beyond this manifestation. If they were to try to pass into further manifestations they wouldn't have the stomach to be able to handle what they would be forced to perceive in order to progress to their most absolute possibilities. Or rather, they *would* have the stomach so as not to be able to handle what they would have to perceive. So that they can encounter and pass beyond these further manifestations, their perception of 'stomach' is removed, thereby eliminating what would otherwise serve as a hindrance in the way of their progression.

"For a soul, coated as it is by retrospective impressions of what it 'should' be and thereby forming itself as it does, the notion of being altered in what *it* perceives as being such a drastic way, namely, in the removal of its stomach, is something of a difficult impression to swallow. The attempt could be made to have an angel simply, what you would perceive as, cut the stomach off the being and scrape out various other impeding organs using some sharpened device. But more than less, a being would have extreme reluctance to their residual self-image ripped apart so abruptly, and the result would be extreme discomfort on the part of the soul that is otherwise unnecessary, combined with a subsequent regeneration of what one's echo of self-conception considers to be something of great importance, a stomach. In order to avoid even the slightest unnecessary annoyance to the soul, and to effect a lasting change to the being necessary for the continuation into succeeding manifestations of Heaven, the method you see before you was created so that said stomach could be in the best way possible removed.

"Take a look at their faces." The driver paused. Tim looked long at the many faces sitting around the table. Many of the faces were contorted in utter disgust and terror, apparently as a result of their meal. Some of the faces were, much to his disbelief, in a state of even neutrality as though they were

70

seated in the most perfectly tranquil, normal, contented situation that they could possibly find themselves in. Most of the faces had expressions anywhere in between the two extremes of joy and disgust, more often leaning toward disgust than not. A handful of the faces, however, were virtually elated, as though the situation of being served bowls heaped with worms was the most blissful, joyous, ecstatic thing there could possibly be, and absolutely nothing out of the ordinary.

As Tim felt he had fairly well exhausted his study of the various facial expressions surrounding the table, he was a moment or two away from looking up to the driver expectantly when, before he had time to even begin to turn his head, the driver began to speak again. "Keep looking, Tim. Watch the *manner* in which they accept their food."

Tim took the scene in as a whole. Tola'El reached the very long wooden spoon he held toward the back wall, alive with multi-colored worms, and scooped up a massive glop of mud that looked to be more worm than mud. He then emptied the contents of the spoon into empty bowls one by one. After filling thirty or so bowls, the spoon being apparently empty, Tola'El scooped another spoonful of worms and mud from the back wall. Tim watched this process many times for many minutes. For a table filled with tens of thousands of diners, Tola'El was very quick in his work, and Tim noticed that no sooner did a being consume the final worm in its bowl than did Tola'El practically fly to that being and refill its bowl.

Watching Tola'El work was a sight to behold, and captured Tim's interest for many refills of the spoon before he finally turned his attention away from Tola'El and toward those who were eating what Tola'El provided. The beings that looked mortified to be eating what they ate *did* eat, but very slowly, very reluctantly, and they twitched and contorted all over, *a lot*. The bellies of those beings with looks of disgust strewn across their faces had abdomens that looked to be completely whole and intact. In a similar manner, those passive, perfectly calm beings without a fear or joy in the world, and appearing to eat in a manner more or less calmly also had bellies one hundred percent intact. The bellies of those overjoyed beings, unlike the beings of those who looked at every worm as though it was the most vile thing God could concoct, had bellies that were rapidly being eaten away by the brown substance trickling down their exposed insides. Those whose facial expressions registered every degree between the two extremes were affected according to nearness or farness to joy in how they received their meals. Those who looked overjoyed to be eating their feast, as though their bowl of multi-colored worms were actually a bowl of rainbow sherbet, gladly scooped worm after worm into their mouths and physically appeared to be basically in a state of deep, vigorous rapture as sections of their bellies went missing. It seemed that the more happy and joyous and peaceful and in love the being, the more of their stomach region tended to be absent.

One being that looked like a man had a sizeable section of his stomach missing despite minor indicators that ever-so-slightly he wasn't enjoying his meal. When this man shuddered after eating several worms, however, Tim noticed that unlike others whose stomachs were slowly but noticeably being eaten away by that same sort of brown acid-like substance dripping and trickling down through their exposed insides, this man not only didn't produce this brown acidic substance, but almost imperceptibly his stomach began to regenerate. He noticed the same phenomenon in other beings handling their meals close to, but with less than, perfect enjoyment and apparent exuberance, be it with a hint of dislike *or* tranquility.

One being, apparently female, looked as though about half of her stomach had been eaten away. After having finished a bowl, however, glancing down and shrieking as though with horror to see the state her 'body' was in, the missing portion of her stomach rematerialized instantly. As the woman resumed bringing worm to mouth, her hand shaking noticeably, one worm after the next almost dropping off her spoon before finding its way into her mouth, Tim noticed that her stomach did not resume its former gradual dissolution.

Watching this now nervous woman concentrating with all her being to try to again regain composure while eating her meal, he observed another being that looked like a woman stand up. He had briefly noted this woman's face earlier as he had gazed around at the various faces, as being one of the few faces that was to all appearances perfectly happy and joyful. Now, as she arose from the table, Tim was struck by what he saw. This woman was fairly tall, had round, full breasts and round, full hips. Her waist was slender, her hair of medium length and golden-blonde. Her face was beautiful and she walked with her head held high, her expression composed and full of grace, joy, happiness, and love. The characteristic that stood out loudly amidst the rest of her features, however, was that this stately creature of such beauty and magnificence had a great space where her stomach should otherwise have been.

Glancing quickly back to other beings that he had noticed previously as being the most happy of the many sitting at the table, he saw what he had expected to see. Those who ate most joyously were those whose stomachs disappeared at the quickest rates, and whose stomachs were far more absent than those of the others sitting around the table.

Looking back to the woman who had so recently arisen from the table, Tim watched as she made her way through the worms back toward the path that had formerly brought Tim to this manifestation of Heaven. As she arose, initially the woman's insides had appeared to be in a rather exposed state. Tim noted, though less than enthusiastic to do so and perpetually wishing that his present form would allow him to vomit, that he could clearly see the woman's remaining organs, moist, and apparently in working order despite a thin, brown, translucent residue that seemed to remain from the substances that had brought her to the state she was currently in. As she began walking toward the path through Heaven, he noticed that as she walked, her insides were slowly becoming less visible. By the time she passed him, where before her internal organs were completely visible, now there was an opaque gold coating of some sort covering her insides that allowed only a very subtle outline of some of the larger remaining organs to be seen.

Tim watched the woman as she walked through the worms, her hips swaying with every step, until she disappeared finally into the layer of clouds that stood between the paths and the third manifestation of Heaven. As he began to turn back toward the table, he noticed that closer to the clouds there seemed to be many short forms spread across the worms, but from the distance at which he stood he couldn't quite make out what they were. He turned his attention back to the table. He looked at the table, the people sitting there, Tola'El serving those at the table, and finally to the driver after he couldn't find anything else to observe. He looked to the driver with expectation and began to think about asking the driver a question that formed in his head, but then thought better of it, catching on to the fact that he seemed rarely to need to vocalize his thoughts to make them known to the driver.

As expected, no sooner did his gaze rest on the driver then did the driver begin to speak. "You have already been informally introduced to Tola'El and told something about his work. This cave in which we stand is his home and dwelling. He works full time, so to speak. Tola'El is the keeper not just of the substance for beings-in-transition intake, which you perceive as worms, but he is also the inspired creator for the Earth's processing of food and soil upkeep system. That is to say, the very worms that inhabit so many gardens that we currently find ourselves shin-deep in. Feel honored to stand in the sanctuary of the guardian of that created for the transmutation of soil and soul alike.

"You noticed, quite rightly, that those of mistaken passions were unaffected by the consumption of their meals, save for whatever external emotional affectations they manifested. You see, the worms they eat, child, are of a certain substance unlike those you stand amidst. As you can see, those affected so greatly mistakenly cannot seem to process any lasting change internally.

"The composition of the worms he serves these Heaven-bound is imbued with a substance that can allow, under the right circumstances, for the successful transmutation of self-conceived-residual-echo into a form more conducive for progression through subsequent manifestations of Heaven. This works due to the quality of the substance contained within these said, what appear to you now as, super-vivid poly-colored sacred-transmuters-o-da-false-into-dee-true.

"As you have already perceived, those of unbalanced temperament cannot receive the gift of transformation that

74

these critters have the ability to provide. Those of positive temperament, however, are transformed with ease depending on how truly balanced with oneself and one's environment one is. Just as there is no reason to cry about a cup of spilled milk, so also there is no reason to be at odds with the inevitable, and it is only through accepting the discomfort that goes along with transformation into a form better suited to experience further transformations that one may truly progress while following the path they have chosen.

"While every once in a while one finds themselves in this manifestation before they are ready, take a brief look, catch a slight whiff, at most try a worm, any of which will cause those not yet suited for such a place to vomit and be sent back into a body, it is fairly rare that one not prepared to go further eventually finds their way here.

"The key to the substance of these worms has to do with their interaction with the substance of emotion produced by one's echo of self-conception, which in effect causes the materialization and sustenance of that echo of self-conception. In other words, the echo causes the echo through consistency of the being's emotive state. When the substance of the worms combines with the substance of the emotions, the substance of the worm is overtaken and dissolved into oblivion, and therefore cannot have the effect for which it was originally designed. When there is some semblance of positivity to the state of a being's emotions, however, the substance of the worm can begin, to some extent, to come through, beginning the transformation process. And when a being's emotions have become completely positive to the notions both of eating something dramatically pleasant *or* unpleasant, depending on the frame of reference of a particular being, and, losing one's stomach, the worms, upon transformation post-ingestion, can fully turn into the acid-like substance designed to eliminate an unnecessary and false sense of what you perceive as being their stomachs.

"Once the transformation of the stomach is complete, the exposed organs are temporarily coated so that one's echo of self-conception has the illusion of protection against threats it is not yet capable of understanding are not present along its journey.

"On a whole, the process is very beautiful, culminating with a heightened degree of serenity that is essential for progression through the Heavenly realm."

Of all adjectives he might have picked to describe what he saw, "beautiful" was not the first to leap to Tim's mind. Disagreements about aesthetic appeal aside, having observed the process the driver had described himself, he felt he understood the driver's words fairly well. Nevertheless, he still couldn't help but feel slightly confused by the time the driver had come to the end of his speech.

As Tim mulled these thoughts around in his mind, staring blankly at the driver, the driver began to speak again. "Well lad, you've seen what you've needed to see. Let's be moving along now, eh?"

And so they turned around and, sleshing and sweshing and squishing through the sea of worms at their feet, slowly, they made their way toward the clouds.

As they were walking, Tim noticed again the short forms that appeared closer to the clouds as the woman had left the manifestation. As he grew closer to these shapes, he was able to make out that they seemed to be people sitting in lotus positions atop the worms. Several feet later, this supposition was confirmed. There, closer than not to the clouds, were in fact a hundred or two men and women scattered sporadically before the clouds, apparently in deep meditation. "As you can see," spoke the driver, "they can be found in all manifestations, though you will find that their numbers grow thinner the farther onward one goes."

They stopped for a brief moment to watch these beings almost floating atop the worms, sitting in what looked to be a deep state of relaxed focus. Tim noted that several of these beings he had the distinct feeling he had seen before, and considered in what way their impressions of what surrounded him might differ from his own.

After a moment or two of such contemplation, Tim and the driver continued walking toward the clouds. He was happy to feel the sandy, muddy feeling turn into a gravely, muddy feeling and then to continue to feel coarser ground underfoot as they made their way out of the manifestation. He was even happier to finally feel the cool stones caress the bare arches of his feet. When he felt the dry, grainy consistency that followed, as well as the cool, crisp dampness of the clouds brushing over and past his cheeks, he began feeling a great deal of relief. Upon coming out of the clouds, the smoothness and relative gleam of gold showing under the ever-thinning worms brought Tim elation, and when his second foot found its way out of the worms and onto the first step of the bus, he found himself completely relieved and able, once again, to fathom relaxation.

The door of the bus shut, and moments later, he could feel soft vibrations as the bus awoke to bring him further on his journey.

Book 6
Manifestation 4: I Love OO? Goodbye!

Five minutes or so, the bus rolled down the path of gold when the driver uttered the inevitable. "Welcome to the fourth manifestation of Heaven!"

The slithy, slimy feeling of worms crawling through his toes and around the lower portions of his legs still tingled on Tim's skin and through his mind. He hadn't yet had time to fully calm himself from his previous experience and attain any manner of relaxation, so he was a little startled that they had already reached the next manifestation. He wasn't too taken aback, however. He would have liked to have spent a little time preparing himself for whatever he would see next, but after a moment of reflection, he remembered that it had taken a while to get to the real substance of the previous manifestation after initially entering it. He figured he might still have some window of opportunity left to try to untie some of the remaining knots in his muscles, apparently the only parts of his "body" completely unaffected from the moment he stepped onto the bus, before he would see whatever there would be for him to "see."

As these thoughts flowed through his head, a heat suddenly arose. He perceived a subtle lightness growing rapidly, despite the still relative darkness pierced periodically by the less than overpowering light given off by the torches. Ahead in the distance he saw an almost imperceptible red glow.

At first the glow was so light that he was scarcely sure it was present. The further the bus went, however, the brighter the glow grew and the lighter the cave became. He also noticed that as the bus moved forward, he felt continually warmer.

For another minute or two things continued to get brighter, lighter, redder, and, not without causing some apprehension, hotter. He noticed a turn coming that seemed to conceal the rest of the glow; he realized that there were no longer any torches.

These thoughts beginning to connect in his mind, the driver spoke. "Keep your senses about you as we take this next turn, sonny-boy."

The bus turned the corner, and Tim felt a wave of heat crash against him. Shadows danced on the clouds, the water became luminous and reflective, and the golden path turned a thick crimson, as though the bus traveled now upon two parallel rivers of blood. Flames could be seen lapping up under and over the clouds that floated along either side of the bus. "Nowhere else, I think," said the driver with a sly grin upon his lips, "will you see flames for *fuel*."

Tim looked down the road and saw no end, nor turns, in the distance. All he saw were the eerily white clouds with shadows dancing upon them, the mirror-like strip of water glowing into the distance, and the stretches of blood without end upon which the bus now rode. Licking at the sides of the road, flames could be seen as far as the eye could reach. Frustrated by the heat, and suddenly confused and uncertain about the smokeless ballet of shadow, reflection, and fire spread before him without any apparent end or anything else to be seen, he was simultaneously relieved and nervous when he finally did notice something that seemed to almost imperceptibly set apart the walls ahead.

Initially, just like the glow, it was barely noticeable; barely a speck on either side of the walls of the cave in the distance, just above the flames. And the flames got bigger as the bus drew closer. And the "specks" grew longer as the bus moved further.

Suddenly the windows of the bus began to lower. Through Tim flashed a cold terror mixed with boiling anger and confusion, all swirling together with the heat of the fire which instantly flooded the interior of the bus as the protection the windows gave was removed. He yelled in a fit of terror, anger, and bewilderment, *"Are you nuts? We'll be cooked alive!"*

The driver looked over at Tim and replied with an exquisite calmness, "Relax, kiddo. I understand you may be a wee bit taken aback as you perceive the temperature to rise a bit, but try to remember, your body isn't exactly in your control for the moment--and for that matter, not exactly subject to the laws of nature you would mistakenly apply to your current set of circumstances. Do be kind enough to sit back and try to relax. I've told you before, you've only yourself to blame if you're not enjoying the ride. Now do be a good lad and keep your ears attentive, will you?"

As the driver uttered these final words, Tim noticed a hum, almost like a warped and twisted form of people chattering from somewhere in front of him. He also noticed that the speck he had seen growing in the distance now had some semblance of a more definable form. Just above the highest flames, not far above the tops of the clouds, a sort of ribbon-like form, not unlike a strip of film, began to take shape.

This strip grew quickly now, the bus apparently moving toward it with great speed. The sound coming from up ahead grew louder and louder. The heat from the flames flooded through the bus, causing him greater discomfort by the passage of every fractured fragment of time.

The strip filled more of his sight by the second as it simultaneously elongated rapidly. The noise grew as though a hand was slowly rotating the dial of an amplifier, his ears beginning to hurt as the sound of jumbled voices swirled at intense volumes through his head. The strip and the bus were now rushing to meet each other at what seemed like an incredible velocity. That which he could for the moment only discern as a vague shape and cacophonous uproar pounding inside of his ears would soon be beside the bus.

Tim felt a pressure within his head, as though it would soon explode from the unbearable blaring and heat, when finally the front end of the strip met with the front of the bus, and suddenly the bus slowed to a crawl, practically coming to a full standstill. The strip moved by practically unnoticeably, and the sounds that he was certain would split his head but a moment ago died down to a comparatively light murmur of several conversations taking place around him at once.

Tim looked out before him, then turned his head to look to either side. On each side of the cave was a long strip of small rooms, every one enclosed by what appeared to be glass. He could see that within the rooms, the walls dividing one room from the next were black. As the back of each of these rooms was a white door with a silver knob, set inside a wall of what seemed to be crystal-clear glass.

The light sounds of multiple conversations taking place at once came to him from all sides, but he was able to make out the conversations taking place closest to the bus most clearly despite the presence of what seemed like hundreds of others. In the closest room to his right, he saw an old woman with a smile on her face and a younger man with an incandescent loop hovering over his head, a big concave layer of bright gold where he would normally have anticipated seeing the lower part of his torso, barely revealing the various remaining organs beneath, and a look on his face that simultaneously embodied rage, fear, and disgust.

In the room to his left was a man and a woman, both of whom looked to be in their mid to early thirties. The man was apparently calm with a concerned look on his face, but the woman, with a halo hovering over her head and a lower torso of gold much like the man in the parallel room, was crying hysterically and looked hurt and confused.

He noted that the rooms he could see ahead of the bus appeared to have similar configurations, though each room contained a unique pair of individuals. As he turned his attention to the nature of the conversation taking place to his right he felt himself wishing to be anywhere but in the midst of these flames arising all around him.

The older woman was speaking when Tim turned his head toward the conversation taking place in that room. "Darling, you know I love you. It's just that I think you ought to acknowledge that your father was in fine health before you met that little whore you came to call your wife. I mean, you couldn't have *known* that marrying her would in any way contribute toward your father's heart failure. I'm just saying that if not for you, I surely would have lived longer and I certainly wouldn't have had to spend my last years living so alone and frightened, dying, knowing my greatest creation brought my greatest sufferings. I love you, dear, I just don't think you've come to terms with some of the mistakes you've made yet."

The younger man had a look of pain on his face so severe that had his fingers and toes been severed and his hands and feet placed in salt water, it could not have been worse. In a voice of sheer rage, the young man yelled at the old woman, "I've apologized and apologized. I love you, why are you being so cruel to me? I didn't know I was causing you such pain. I never meant to cause you such pain. I didn't mean to hurt you or Dad. I can't do anything to change what happened now! I can't change it! I can't change it! I can't change it! I didn't mean to hurt you. What can I do? What can I do to make you stop hating me? What can I do for you just to hold me again now that we've finally found each other again? I'm sorry. I'm so fucking sorry! What do you want from me? Please tell me what to do, what to say! What can I do to make it good again? I'm sorry!"

Calmly, with great concern on her face, the woman responded, "Now son, I know you're sorry, but you have to learn from your mistakes, just like I had to learn to cope with the burden of raising you for all those years after the hours of excruciating torment I spent giving birth to you. Just like I had to learn to cope with the dark void left in me by your father's death that came so early, killing me slowly and painfully second by second over the next fifteen years that followed. It's really just that I don't think you fully realize all the pain you brought to us by marrying that little slut you thought of as a wife. And think of those children you left fatherless. If you hadn't been so arrogant, thinking you knew the city *so* well, they never would have had to watch you die for the pathetic seven dollars and forty-two cents you had stuffed inside your wallet, and that cheap, fake watch of yours. Of course you weren't even half the father *yours* was, but you were at least, probably, better than nothing, and now, because of your thick little skull, they won't have even what little bit of support you could have given them. It's just shameful some of the mistakes you've made, that's all. I'm here to help you come to grips with those silly little errors of judgment you've made, my sweet child." The old woman said these last words with a beneficent smile beaming from her visage toward her son, whose face was twisting into ever-increasing horror and confusion.

Before the woman's son began another volley of uncertain, pained, angry response, Tim looked away from the conversation with a sense of disgust and turned his focus toward the conversation taking place in the room parallel to the one within which he had just listened.

The woman was speaking as well as she could through a veritable waterfall of tears cascading down her face from crimson eyes. In sobs resonating a hysteria she tried to conceal despite herself she cried, " . . . so many times! You told me you loved me so many times! Was it a lie all along? For so many years? I left everybody behind gladly, and was so happy, together, with you. It . . . it was all a lie?"

The man's voice responded calmly, gently, "Of course it wasn't a lie, my one true love. I slept with those other women only because they were so much better in bed, and you just didn't have that knack for fucking quite like every other of my companions did."

"Fucking?" Her anger was barely revealed beneath her other layers of despondence and distress, "Was that all it was to you? F-Fucking? You told me you were completely in love with me. With *only* me. We made love. I . . . I thought we were making love. Your mere touch and I . . . You said there couldn't be any other. Fucking? Was that all I . . . we . . . *us* . . . Fucking?"

"But you are the only one for me, my love," the gentleman's voice was consoling. "They were only to keep me satisfied sexually, and to provide a little intellectual stimulation every once in a while. I love you, my darling. You *are* my one and only, you know that. But I deserved some kind of intelligent intercourse with *someone,* didn't I? I needed *some* sort of sexual enjoyment, didn't I?"

She began to scream from behind the flow of her tears. "I left all my friends, my family to be with you! I . . . I thought we were so . . . I was so . . . happy. Why are you saying all these horrible things? We were so . . . why would you . . . how could you . . ."

"Now, now, my love." The man had a graceful smile on his lips and spoke in a soothing tone of voice. "You didn't have to come with me. You didn't have to make those sacrifices. It seemed rather stupid to me that you would follow me around everywhere like a dog, but you did, and that just added to the cuteness of having you tag along. It just added to what I found so endearing about you. That kind of naiveté was so fun to have around, it was wonderful to always have company like *yours* within arms' reach, my love."

Tim grimaced to hear this constant stream of apparent cruelty being spoken.

As the man spoke, his words faded quickly into the background with the sound of the chatter of hundreds of others having similar conversations. New voices could suddenly be heard clearly, and Tim became aware that his window was presently closest to the next set of parallel rooms.

Now a younger woman was berating an older one for never paying enough attention to her growing up, and an old man critiqued to no end by a younger man for never having made anything out of his life. Tim looked down the road, and as far as he could see, the walls were lined with more rooms, a unique couple in every room. In the next set of rooms a woman was begging a man to stop drinking as he denied his habit through alcohol-soaked saliva being spat at her after every sip he took from an apparently endless supply of liquid out of a bottle in a bag. In the parallel room, a man was asking a woman as politely as he could through his tears to stop hitting him as she denied profusely the golf club she swung repeatedly at his head. In the next set of rooms a man was slapping a haloed woman repeatedly with the back of his hand while having sex with her twin sister from behind; on the other side, a man was asking a woman for money as she shouted the question of whether he was nuts, and further whether or not he could see that in her clothing of nakedness she had absolutely no place she could possibly conceal an extra dollar for him, nor would she where she could. In another room an old woman screamed at a young man sitting nonchalantly in a chair to please kiss her. In another a woman was talking her head off about exploits that were obviously lies at the young man slowly rocking himself back and forth at her feet, who every so often muttered under his breath, trying desperately to get a word in edgewise. A young girl without a stomach was crying to her young uncle sitting at a table laden with food to please help her with a puzzle as he continued to offer her a sandwich. A young man sitting at a desk, being screamed at by a young woman with a halo for him to give her a note of love as he casually waved a piece of paper, in the end saying with a fat, shit-eating grin on his face, "What, this old thing?" A young, otherwise attractive naked woman slowly slicing her skin with a razor blade before a golden-gutted young man weeping in horror and disbelief, grabbing at her arms, wrestling with her, and begging her to stop hurting herself as she slashed at herself merrily as though picking flowers. So far as Tim could discern, in every room in this "manifestation of Heaven," another, whom the first apparently loved a great deal, was completely unwilling to change a pattern of abuse and was verbally, or otherwise psychologically, assaulting the first.

Tim looked into each room apprehensively as he felt wave upon wave of heat from the flames outside the bus rushing over him. He felt an abundance of sympathy for those gutless ones bearing the cruelty of these who were apparently people they had loved most while alive, and felt frustrated that they were subjected to what occurred to him as the cruelest treatment one could be subjected to. Watching all of these beings with tears in their eyes and anger in their throats, he half expected that he would become one of them in short time if the driver decided suddenly to turn around himself and start accusing him of being the reason he had gotten in the bus crash that had killed him so long ago.

Tim felt the bus begin to speed up very gradually after passing the first couple dozen rooms. He still had more than enough time to catch a strong earful of the next several conversations, despite the increase in the bus's speed. Apparently an older woman was a lousy mother and an old man was completely self-absorbed, though he was less than confident in the opinions of the accusers.

As another dozen more rooms were passed, the bus sped up again. Again he listened, this time to a sister denouncing a brother and a young man mocking the thin-skinned secrets of his best friend. He actually felt some sympathy for the sad young boy without a stomach as his supposed friend made fun of him because of his sexual orientation. Upon passing these rooms, again the bus gained momentum, and again he listened to the apparently unbecoming badgering of one being by another, whom was evidently a central image of love in the eyes of the one being berated. Try as he might, he was becoming less and less relaxed with the heat around him.

By the fourth dozen pairs of rooms, he was starting to have difficulty following the conversations due to the speed of the bus. By the eighth dozen pairs of rooms he was able to get a good sense of only one of the conversations taking place, and the heat was becoming once again a considerable distraction. By the sixteenth dozen pairs of rooms, the gist of any conversation was just outside his ability to distinguish virtually anything being said. By the twenty-third dozen pairs of rooms it was useless to try to discern information anymore, and the chatter of all the conversations taking place around him began to merge into one another, again creating an uneasy, noisome convergence of sound not entirely pleasant to the ears and causing him incredible discomfort, especially when coupled with the heat of the flames flowing in and out of the open windows of the bus. The frustration of hearing a cacophony of voices raised in malice and insecurity mixed with the ever-increasing speed of the bus, along with the heat that almost seemed, again, to be increasing, caused the fragile balance of discomfort and sanity he was trying with the entirety of his being to maintain to become that much more fragile and loom on the border of giving way in entirety to the anxiety building within him with every passing moment.

The bus rolled down the road quickly enough that he could no longer make out any of the conversations, but slowly enough that he could still clearly distinguish the faces of those verbally or otherwise causing consternation, and those who listened and saw with tears in their eyes. He moved his head back and forth rapidly and repeatedly while trying to glimpse each couple speeding by the windows of the bus, and he did this on the verge of what felt to be an imminent anxiety-driven meltdown. The heat, the voices, the strong feeling of frustration fueling his inability to alleviate the amount of suffering all around him and, indeed, *within* him, caused him to feel as though the entire world he was perceiving was being plunged into him as a pressurous mass of imploding reality, and he was on the brink of losing whatever modicum of composure he still clung tenaciously to when the driver's words suddenly resonated within his head. "How long were you planning on holding it in?"

"What?" said Tim, looking up toward the driver, suddenly realizing the absence of all sounds save for that of his own voice making a feeble reply.

"Well, look at you, son," responded the driver with a look of warmth and sympathy radiating from a face peeking at him from over the driver's shoulder.

Becoming aware of himself, Tim found his body huddled in an unfortunately not altogether unfamiliar position, the fetal position. As he began unfolding his body and attempting to sit up straight again, he responded to the driver's inquiry. "The conversations of these people, they're horrible. I must have tensed without even realizing it somewhere between the heat and listening to what some of these people were saying to the others. Why are these people being abused this way if this is *Heaven*?"

"Well, I've told you before." The driver spoke with the same kind grin beaming forth from his face. "You'll have the best trip possible by relaxing.

"As far as your question goes, well, let's begin with what I've told you all along. Do try to remember that all that you see is approximate at best, and that as you are, you couldn't even begin to fathom the reality of what you're in the process of perceiving. That being said, look to those with whom I'm sure you've been inclined to be sympathizing, those with the halos and lacking bellies." Tim looked into a room at his right and saw a young girl with a halo above her head, a large gold indentation revealing a hint of organs underneath, and a look on her face filled with dread coupled with water falling from her eyes.

"These are the ones," continued the driver, "who have progressed through the first three manifestation of Heaven one way or another. It should be noted that at this point in the journeys of those traveling through Heaven, it is very rare that reincarnation takes place. Up until the previous manifestation, reincarnation is not infrequent or so rare, but those who make it this far tend to have a different kind of resolve than those who are able to progress to the third manifestation. There are some who reincarnate shortly after making it this far, but it is very, very rare, and to see any being reincarnated in further manifestations is practically unheard of. It happens sometimes because a highly evolved being is needed to prevent some manner of catastrophic happening on the earth, or some such thing. That a being turns back at this point or later in the journey, however, there aren't many instances. Really, any being who makes it this far would probably spend any subsequent lives dealing with the same basic problems endlessly on Earth, and there is no reason why that being cannot simply take the same several lifetimes to solve the same problem here, without the distractions that mundane life held for them when that mundane life was needed to get them to the point they find themselves at now. It just wouldn't be practical.

"Now, those causing these 'journeyers' so much trepidation are projections of the person whom in life the soul felt its strongest bond with or connection to. The connection these beings felt with these people in life was so strong, you see, that a sizeable resonance was created within these beings' residual echoes of self-conception, and are a sizeable portion of the excess of that which these beings passing through Heaven still needlessly-to-the-point-of-impediment cling to. Since the process of progressing through Heaven entails transmutation of one's form into a truer and more essential state, in this manifestation the echo of said 'loved one' is used to change the form of the journeyer to be able to enter further manifestations, where the form of the being would otherwise be detrimental in forthcoming manifestations, much like having a belly would be detrimental to progression after the third.

"The nature of the progression through Heaven, dear child, is a solitary one. In order for these beings to be able to go further they must have an established and concrete focus of mind. The echoes these beings have of these loved ones is so strong that they interfere with the clarity necessary to perceive the reality of their situations, to such a high degree that these residual echoes must be released or reformed so as to allow for a more objective perspective to be able to move onward.

"These beings love and desire to be with their loved ones so much, you see, that they endure lifetimes of abuse from the images of said people so as to be able to share space with them at all. Initially these souls are elated just to be abused by these beings whom they so cherish, and this inclination to forsake their own value and purpose is precisely what must be eliminated before they are capable of moving on to succeeding manifestations of Heaven.

"There's a saying you may have heard on Earth that might be familiar to you. 'If you love someone, let them go.' For you to *begin* to conceive of the reality of this manifestation, let us say that this is the ultimate test of that very principle. In order for these souls to truly express their love for those people whom they hold onto so strongly in their conceptions of themselves, indeed, for them to truly love themselves, they must let go of those whom they want nothing more than to be near, but who wind up being the very obstacle keeping them from progressing further. To move always further on one's journey is a form of love as action. As the opposite of love manifests as fear, fear manifests opposite action, in this case, as stagnation. These souls fear being absent from their loved ones, and thus will take any form of abuse just to be near them. Look." As the driver said this, he pointed toward the window closest to Tim.

Tim noticed first that the bus was no longer moving forward. Looking out of the window right next to him, on his right, he saw that the bus had stopped next to another of the rooms. He could not hear the conversation, but an old man was waving his arms, gesturing emphatically, and a girl who appeared to be in her mid-twenties was looking at the old man almost with a smile on her face. It surprised Tim to see this girl with a halo over her head and no stomach even almost smiling, when all the others had looked so broken to be speaking to one whom they apparently loved. The old man stopped talking. This girl, with radiance upon her face and something very close to a gentle smile upon her lips, looked at the old man. As a single tear fell from the corner of her right eye, she appeared to utter three short words. She placed her hand under the old man's chin, kissed his right cheek, and turned to face the back wall. She turned the silver knob of the door in the wall, opened the door, and walked through. The door shut behind her, and as she walked out of Tim's view a look of recognition crossed instantly over the old man's face, and he dissolved into thin air, a new couple materializing as the last traces of his image faded from sight; a beautiful young woman and a young man with a ring of light above his head, a large golden indentation where his stomach should be, and a look on his face beaming with pure elation.

"That shine in his eyes won't last long," began the driver again. "The flames hasten the friction of emotion experienced by the journeyer. The quicker they come to total breakdown and a desire to get away, the quicker they can move forward on their journey. With the aid of a little fire, breaking away can take centuries, where otherwise it might take millennia. The heat helps one fuse one's soul together into the more pure primal state of love it seeks to achieve by making this journey forward. The heat breaks apart the uncomposed illusion of composure so that the truer elements of one's being may find itself and bring itself together to become a higher level of being, inseparable and closer to the truest nature of what the soul actually is and strives ultimately to be. When one has brought oneself into this more solidified mode of being, one can then leave this manifestation and continue further."

The bus started rolling down the path again.

"She uttered the last words that most utter before leaving this manifestation, 'I love you.' Either they say that, or leave in silence. There tends not to be many variations on the form their exits take.

"It takes great courage to walk away from that which is harmful in the guise of something apparently necessary. It takes even more courage to leave the safety of that harm and leave oneself blindly in the hands of fate to carry one further on a journey in which the destination is unknown. It takes love to keep moving on. It takes love to let go. It takes faith to take that unknown path, that the path might lead one to something somehow better."

After speaking these last words, the driver turned back toward the road ahead, and instantly Tim's head was filled with the sounds of loud chatter from all sides as he suddenly became acutely aware of a feeling of being roasted alive, perceiving flame licking the frames where the windows of the bus should have been. He perceived the velocity of the bus once again moving at such a speed that the rooms on either side flew past in a blur.

He did his best to let the waves of heat roll over him, *through* him. He released himself to the sounds he could not stop from pounding through his skull. Immediately and automatically tensing as the bus bounded down the road, he saw tension arise within himself, and he did his best to release himself to the journey he was on. Ever so slightly he relaxed his form to conform naturally to the seat he was in, accepted his surroundings for being beyond his ability to control, yielded to the will of the bus, and saw clearly that he could not do anything but. As the bus traveled down the road, he perceived the rooms passing by. As the pairs of people blurred in front of his vision, he contemplated what the driver had told him about the manifestation and began to feel at ease with their fates.

————————

Tim reflected on his travels thus far and contemplated that much of his journey was spent relearning the simple act of relaxation. He reflected on what he had seen and wondered just how long the ride would last. Considering then the destination of this trip he was on, he noticed that he wasn't particularly anxious for the journey to end.

Book 7
Manifestation 5: No Skin Off One's No-see (a.k.a. Knows)

Remembering once again how to let his muscles loosen, it felt as though hours drifted by while tens of thousands of people seemed to pass beside his window. Accepting the fates of those he saw encased in glass, Tim relaxed into a calm, introspective, meditative state virtually unperturbed by the intensity of the heat or the persistent noise of chatter surrounding him.

He felt as though he was falling, deeper and deeper, entering into various states of relaxation, the noise slowly leaving him as he descended more and more into an internal world of silence and serenity. He became aware of silence surrounding him and was drawn toward the light sound of one of his own thoughts. This thought led to another and quickly his thoughts returned him again to the sound of the chatter around him, but now it seemed to be sounding strongest from behind.

Opening his eyes, he saw five rooms pass by very quickly, followed by cave wall. The flames rapidly diminished lower and lower, until finally they disappeared altogether and the heat was replaced by a refreshing cool, crisp dampness supplied by the clouds hovering next to the window. The tumult of the chatter of voices now entirely behind him subsided to a slight murmur, then ceased entirely.

The windows of the bus rose. He found the subsidence of heat and noise tremendously relieving and breathed a sigh accordingly as an organic relaxation passed through him. Without turning his head, the driver's voice could be heard clear, "Welcome to the fifth manifestation of Heaven."

A mild red glow illuminated the cave in the distance. Against the light of the glow, Tim saw a very small figure moving toward the light. As the bus moved forward the light grew and became brighter. The figure also grew and became almost easy to recognize as what looked like a person walking toward the light ahead.

A minute later the bus was very close to the source of the light, and the person walking upon the path of water could clearly be discerned to be a woman. He noticed that the woman's shape looked somehow familiar, then realized that she must be the same woman he had seen leave the last manifestation. Looking down at her feet, he was struck by the fact that she didn't seem to be making any ripples on the water upon which she walked. Glancing up haphazardly, the wonder he felt at seeing the woman's feet making no ripples upon the surface of the water was soon replaced in his mind by an even greater sight after which he wondered. This woman was missing something that he hadn't noticed missing when she had left the previous manifestation. Though he couldn't quite see clearly due to the length of her hair, he could swear that she now had no shoulders. Whenever her hair flowed away from the place where her shoulders should have been, he caught a glimpse of what seemed to be golden indentations of sorts. Her arms still swung like anybody's who was taking a walk, as though connected to her torso by skin and muscle and bone, but she apparently lacked what could be definitively described as shoulders, and a kind of radiance appeared to surround the absent shoulder area.

"No longer does she have need of the form of courage that it took to stand up for herself," spoke the driver rather suddenly, catching Tim off-guard just as he began once again to fall into the habit of assuming the privacy of his own thoughts. "The courage to stand tall for oneself is, at least as far as your limited abilities of perception are concerned, represented here as being contained within the shoulders. What you didn't notice as this woman walked away, after stepping outside the door, was that along with the image of her father dissolving, so too dissolved her shoulders. In truth, the two were the same. The cause was the effect, and the solution being found, the reality more clearly being perceived, what you perceived was that that which was left behind was in actuality a part of her being transmuted and integrated into a firmer form and higher degree of substance within her, enabling the rest of her being to progress further to be refined further. As *her* being changes, so in some form does that change appear to you, in this case, in the form of her shoulders."

———

The bus was now very close to the woman, slowly following behind her. Tim watched her walk on the water. The bus stopped and the door of the bus opened. The driver said, "Let's go," as he stood up and began stepping down the top step of the bus's stairs. Tim stood up and walked toward the door quickly to keep up with the driver.

———

Stepping off the bus once again, Tim saw the driver walking on the right-hand side of the road of gold, just a few steps ahead of where Tim now stood beside the door of the bus. Walking several feet ahead of the driver was the woman with the halo above her head and the gold where her stomach and shoulders "should" have been.

He ran lightly a couple of steps to catch up to the driver.

They walked in silence on the path of gold a few feet behind the woman walking on the water. They did not walk very long before coming to where the red glow was most discernable through the clouds, filling the cave enough that torches were not needed for several feet in either direction. The woman turned to the left, off the path of water, onto the path of gold, and finally disappeared into the clouds where the red of the glow through cloud shown brightest.

The driver stepped onto the water following after the woman. Tim followed after the driver.

Without giving it a second thought, Tim stepped onto the water with his right foot, completing the intention of his movement with his left. His left foot found its way onto the road of gold on the other side of the middle path when he realized that he was *walking on water*. After this thought ran through his mind he looked back at his right foot still on the path of water. Practically no sooner did he see his foot on the water than *in* the water, for the moment he looked back to marvel at the minor feet of miracle he had performed, his right foot sank down beneath the water's surface.

Tim's foot sank slowly into the water at first, but it happened unexpectedly, and before he could think to get himself to the other side of the water, his leg was already entirely submerged and he was sinking fast. His left foot stayed on the gold, but the rest of him fell into the water. Reflexively, he shot his right hand out to grab onto the golden road while he was falling. He tried to pull himself onto the golden road, but he couldn't get a grip on it at all and the water suddenly seemed to be tugging strongly at him as though it were attempting to pull him in, pull him under.

He got his left hand up onto the gold, but this caused his left foot to fall into the water. He continued trying with all his being to force his hand to friction with the slippery path, but the water grew ever swifter and, despite his best efforts, pulled him ever downward.

The water was sucking him down into itself regardless of the energy he expended to fight being drawn in, and he found his fingers sliding off of the road as his body sank down into the stream. His head submerged as his fingers lost contact with the gold. His fingertips were in the air, ready to sink into oblivion, when he felt them held firmly by a concentrated, friendly warmth. Slowly, he rose straight up through the water, and as his eyes reemerged from the water, he was overjoyed at the sight of the driver helping him to a drier location; his own fingertips apparently pinched by those of the driver.

"Oh ye of little faith!" said the driver with a smirk on his face. He raised Tim to where he himself stood in the middle of the stream.

Tim felt weightless in the driver's hand and found himself once again standing, this time toe to toe with the driver upon the path of water. With Tim in hand, the driver walked to the left-side path of gold. Tim felt as though his feet glided over the water as the driver pulled him over the water's surface.

Having taken a step and a half, and having brought Tim safely to the other side of the golden path, the driver left him to his own two legs.

"Knowing beyond any doubt that they must travel the middle path ever onward, they are enabled to walk on the water without ever experiencing any fear of falling in. It is the quality inherent to every being walking this path. It is faith. They don't know where the path will lead, and every stop along the way impedes them from continuing onward. But it is these stops that allow them also to move forward. The faith of those in Heaven is challenged at every step along the way, and it is only by enduring and passing through and beyond those challenges to progression that a being may advance, grow, and develop in the ways that are necessary for ever strengthening and reaffirming the faith they need to continue to walk down the middle path, toward further unknown and different manifestations of the place in which they journey. The middle path is the only way they may continue forward through Heaven, and stagnation is not an option. Either a being will progress onward toward that which has been laid before them, or they will regress toward rebirth, but there is no standing still, and only their faith keeps them moving forward since they know not where the road may lead.

"For those who find the path, nothing short of the faith required to walk on water will suffice to go onward. If a being is not in a state suitable for walking the path, they'll quickly sink, be overcome by the currents beneath the water's surface, and submerge. Not being prepared fully to make the journey down the middle path, one must inevitably start again.

"Of course, you must always bear in mind that all of this is a shadow of the truth of where you stand, a metaphor. Remember that the reality of the situation isn't exactly a stroll down your average creek, and that while this serves to show you something of the truth, it cannot possibly show you fully the reality, and to be sure, must mislead you since you can't begin to fathom the truth behind what you perceive. Now! Come along, boy." And with that the driver began walking toward the ruby-hued clouds into which the woman had disappeared a minute or two prior.

Tim looked at the driver for a moment with a mild sense of confusion while trying to assimilate and understand what the driver had said. He stood transfixed by his own thoughts as he watched the driver begin to dissolve into the blood-red wall of cloud in front of him. As the apparent floating sea of crimson immersed the driver beyond sight, he snapped to his senses and rushed toward the fiery mists, lest he be left alone.

———

Tim entered the clouds and found his self to be surrounded by a scarlet world of mist; a cool, crisp, red feeling kissing his cheeks as he passed through to the other side.

He took one step, two steps, three steps, and coming out of the mists quickly realized a true horror facing him as he slowed the pace of his stride to a grudging halt. He stood aghast to behold what stood before him.

Slowly, he took one step, two steps, three steps, and there stood stock still beside the driver. The driver lifted his arm and extended a finger, pointing forward. Tim aligned his gaze to where the driver pointed and saw the woman they had been following, the woman from the previous manifestation, approximately twenty paces ahead of where they now stood, standing, gazing in the direction of all that stood before them.

The woman stood motionless, as though surveying the scene before her, for several seconds. She seemed to be watching; watching and taking in the horrible happenings that lay ahead of her. She stood and watched, but with exquisite composure as though completely unperturbed by what she saw. She then stepped forward.

———

As she started taking *her* first step forward, the driver pushed lightly on Tim's back, and he and the driver also took a step forward. The woman stepped again, and Tim again felt pressure against his back toward the shoulder; they again stepped forward. She stepped a third time, and the pair that stood behind her also took a third step forward.

A fourth step, a fifth step, a sixth step, and Tim's vision of the horror of what lay ahead became all the clearer and more vivid with every subsequent footfall. A seventeenth step, an eighteenth step, a nineteenth step, and he felt the blood-red fire upon his cheeks, upon his face; the pounding of the drums beating in his ears, the screams of those he beheld violently rising over and crashing into those beats, sending pulses of sound through the cave where they all found themselves to be. Step twenty-three, step twenty-four, step twenty-five, and he began to be able to discern the lines in their faces as their faces contorted into each grimace of pain, each flinch of pure agony; lines arising at the corners of their mouths as they issued forth declarations of pain in the wails that were emitted from their throats. Thirty-three, thirty-four, thirty-five, and the woman entered into the outermost circle; a ring of terrors intensifying as one searched within this circle that held all that he couldn't begin to express the revulsion culminating within him to be perceiving. Thirty-nine, forty, forty-one, and Tim and the driver stood before the circle; the outermost part made up of those in anguish, as was the innermost part.

Tim, now still, watched the woman enter within the circle. She passed by those already present as she made her way toward the circle's center. The boundaries of this circle were created by those beings whose places were at the circle's outermost edges. Those inside the circle were just as those forming the perimeter of the ring, and there were apparently thousands of them. At four spots behind the boundary of the circle, as though standing at each "corner" of the circle, were four beings, each of whom stood before and pounded down upon, apparently with all their being, a very large, very loud, drum; sixteen drummers in all.

The woman walked in further. Those whom she walked around and through took one of two forms. Some were like her; a halo over their heads, a big golden groove where one might otherwise have expected to see a stomach, and a similar condition effecting upon their shoulders, or lack thereof. Most of these beings, those like her, were also missing great quantities of skin, or were very scratched up, or somewhat scratched up, or in at least some way or another cut.

The other beings Tim saw were human as far as the shape of their bodies were concerned. Their faces and heads, however, were either horribly disfigured or appeared to resemble the forms of animals. He saw faces of wolves, jackals, hyenas and other beasts that may be found upon earth or otherwise. Their bodies, however, appeared clearly human and whole, without the lightest blemish or even the slightest scrape. All of them were strong and muscular. All of them were somewhat frightening to Tim. All of them held a whip, knife, mallet, razor, or other implement of torture in one of their hands, if not both.

The woman continued walking deeper into the circle as all around her, arms manipulated that which their hands held; their tools finding their ways into what Tim saw as the flesh of those bound to travel deeper into Heaven. Screams filled the air as a jackal took his razor and set to work slowly slicing thin, bloody slivers of skin off one being hunched over what looked almost like a gymnast's pommel horse but lower and without handles to grip. A dog with a long bullwhip rhythmically beat at the flesh of another holding tightly to a rope that hung overhead; the whip striking quickly and with great force, lash, after lash, after lash. A goat-faced being took something resembling a cheese grater to the chest of a being lying on their back; their body contorting in agony under sprays of blood. An ant-faced entity bit at the lower back of one whose legs were half-submerged in the ground.

The ground ran red, flowing down apparently to fuel the fire surrounding it all; the bright red blazes causing sweat to seep from the pores of every being in this cave as the fire itself gave off something of a light red mist; vapors where the blood initially met with the fire. Agony resounded off the walls and flowed to every open ear to create a sick sort of rhythmic dissonance when combined with the beating of the drums and the sound of ripping flesh.

She walked by people stretched across anvils while maggot-faced creatures, scorpion-faced creatures, and centipede-faced creatures used stones to rip at their flesh. Some had thin strips of skin removed by the long, curved, sharp fingernails of a beast with the head of a lamb. Some were having skin scraped off by the top teeth of beings with the heads of lions. All around her long knives slashed down and hands pulled at the flesh where the cuts had been made. Chains flashed, removing flesh along with light showers of blood. The bark of trees was used on some curled over rocks, their bare backs exposed to wood and heat. The lone talon of an eagle held by the hand of a jellyfish-faced being was brought repeatedly into the flesh of others. The repeated stroke of a cat-o-nine tails here, the implementation of live regular-sized scorpions used as tools there. Everywhere surrounding this woman was every conceivable device, and some beyond conception, being used to separate skin from body by beings with the heads of every kind of beast Tim could imagine, and others beyond his worst nightmares.

She walked forward until she came to a being with a head like a peacock. She stood before it and bowed her head. It raised its arm and upon her back descended a whip that had spikes imbedded in it, about an inch apart from each other down the entire length of the leather strip. She immediately released a bloodcurdling shriek of agony, but her face betrayed no horror or dread, only an eerily calm pain. Where the whip had been, a large red welt remained with a long strip of skin hanging at its base, blood dripping down her back, flowing over her buttock, down her leg, and to the ground below. No sooner had the beast raised its whip again, however, than did the welt disappear and the strip of skin fall to the ground below; dissolving into the flow of blood at her feet cascading across the floor toward the sides of the cave.

As Tim watched the various other beings being tortured, he noticed the same phenomenon take place. Arms descended, skin was removed, and blood flowed into the greater tide of red below. In most cases, however, the skin almost immediately rematerialized.

Tim couldn't help but compare the scene in front of him to the one he had witnessed in the third manifestation. Just as before, with most, the skin grew back immediately. Just as before, some had *some* skin partially removed, but even they seemed to have merely a slower rate of regeneration of flesh. A very few had large portions of their muscle structure showing;

no golden covering issued forth to cover the redness of their wounds, however. The only overt change in the physical structure of those whose skin was most heavily removed was a cessation of bleeding several minutes after the muscle had been forced into nakedness.

The beast-headed ones were also attacking the gold of their bellies and shoulders without discrimination. Though the gold coverings didn't disappear, they did seem to get lighter when struck. Those with the most muscle showing had gold coverings that were greatly diminished in the intensity of their golden hue. It was as though the color had been thinned so that rather than a physical layer of protection, what seemed to remain over their internal organs was more like a light golden glow surrounding suddenly very vivid and very exposed livers, spleens, and gallbladders; muscle and bones in the case of lacking shoulders.

While these beings were being struck apparently without any regard for where they were being struck, Tim noticed no mark of abuse on any of their faces, nor did he perceive any violence being perpetrated against their faces. This observation struck Tim as odd, since the rest of the head of these people seemed to be fair game for those with a bestial visage.

––––––––––

Tim watched all that happened before him with sheer terror in his eyes and pure anguish in his ears. He felt as though he would do anything to be able to retch; the sounds of torture and torment reverberating through his skull almost unbearable. At this moment, he wished he was just about anywhere but where he now was. After the previous episodes in his journey, however, and having responded as he had to the previous manifestations, though his skin crawled and he grew hot with the tension of not wanting to see what he was seeing or hear what he was hearing, he couldn't help but notice, nor could he deny, that he was still far more composed than he had been in several other occasions not terribly unlike this one. This thought flashing through his mind as he watched the vision of

Heaven taking place before him helped ease his tensions, if only slightly.

Not unexpectedly, the voice of the driver entered Tim's ears as though in response to his thoughts. "I know it's not a pleasant sight, but as I've told you, and will continue to keep telling you, what you see is but a representation of what you in your ignorance might designate by the word 'truth.' Where before they needed to create strength of being, dissolve their 'stomachs' and shed their 'shoulders,' here they come to be stripped of their 'skin.'"

Tim shuddered a little as the word "skin" left the driver's mouth. He briefly flashed on an image of his own skin being removed as he watched the many forms of torture, or rather "skin removal," taking place in front of him. He shuddered a little more as something in his mind tried to begin to speculate as to what manner of device one of these animals might use on him.

"That is to say," continued the driver, "in the fifth manifestation of Heaven, these beings come to lose the outermost coating of their echo of self-conception, which they view as being their greatest attribute since they perceive that it simultaneously keeps out that which may be potentially dangerous, and keeps in and together in the best way possible those many composite parts which they feel are necessary and requisite for their continued progression—in this case represented as skin.

"In Heaven there is no harm that may arise, and likewise, these extra elements appended to one's being, when carried with them through Heaven, are not only not of utility for continuing on their way, but actually act as a hindrance. For this reason, before one can move forward, they must be rid of this useless and hindering element of their echo of self-conception. Only then can they move on to further manifestations of Heaven.

"Here there are various divine beings created solely for the removal of the skin of those you see before you. These who have made it thus far and whose primary internal spark of reason creates a sincere impulse for progression through Heaven come here to have their skins removed.

"Removal of this element of one's being is never an easy process, however, since the reason these beings retain their skin to begin with is the firmly rooted identity and feelings of necessity they have attached to this particular aspect of their perceived state of self. As a result, as a part of their skin is removed, just like in the third manifestation of Heaven, if they are not ready to fully accept the removal of a part of their skin, the part removed will be regenerated until such time as a being is ready to detach from that aspect they falsely believe to be a part of themselves, and a necessary part at that.

"The gold lining over those parts that have been already removed act almost in lieu of what you would consider to be a sort of replacement or surrogate skin. The gold, as you see it, gives the impression of protection from their perspective to make it easier to progress further. What looks gold to you, to them is perceived as a marker indicative of the level of progression to which they have attained, but also a measure of security. Here, though, their false need of vanity and security gives way to a truer sense of realization of one's truth, or essential being. When a being leaves this place, they leave behind a very large portion of the false layers they previously perceived as being vital to avoid the very pain they ultimately go through to alleviate their burden of a false sense of self, and take further on their journey a clearer perception and form of the truest aspects of their composition."

As the driver finished his speech, Tim was gazing deeply into the circle of horror before him, watching the ripping and slashing and flaying and running of blood that filled the entirety of his field of vision. While thinking about what the driver had just said, and trying to feel at all at ease with what he saw, he noticed a figure begin to move away from a table and an apparently dragon-headed being at the far side of the circle. The figure moved slowly through the throng. It walked first toward the center of the circle. As it reached the center of the circle it began walking out toward the "entrance" of the circle, in front of which Tim was standing.

As this being began walking toward him, he was able to make out more of the details of the being. He first noticed that this person wasn't missing a great deal of skin. There were a couple of obvious places where muscle was showing, mostly on his upper arms, a little on his legs, and most of his neck, but aside from that, it was a far cry from lacking all its skin. The next thing Tim was able to make out was that the figure moving toward him was male.

The man continued to get closer, appearing more clearly with every step. Tim still couldn't make out the man's face, but he could see more of *him*; smaller strips of skin missing from his exposed muscle. He then began to see that while this man's face was still a bit out of focus, it was fully intact despite there being quite a bit of skin missing from the rest of his head. He shuddered at seeing parts of this man's skull exposed. While the gold around this man's stomach and shoulder areas wasn't as light as he had seen on others, it did appear lighter than on those who were missing less skin than this man was.

As the man started leaving the circle, his face finally came fully into view. A long, thin beard grew off his chin, and his face seemed somehow very familiar to Tim.

He searched the man's face. He looked tired and worn-down, but there was almost a glow of vitality somewhere behind the man's eyes. The longer he studied the man's face, the more familiar it seemed to be. It occurred to him that he had seen this face before. He thought about it, and it seemed that perhaps the last time he had seen this man he had been without a beard; and then, at recognition, it was as though something had clicked on in his head and he knew who it was he was looking at.

"Walter!" Tim cried the name with conviction as he experienced a moment of astonishment and great awe. This had been the man he had seen in the second manifestation, who'd passed to the third manifestation without stopping any longer than was necessary to read the sign on the tollbooth.

Tim was somehow set at ease to see a familiar face, even if it was one attached to a body that didn't seem to be doing so well. He knew nothing about the man in front of him, nor had they ever met. Even so, he felt a bond with this man. He felt a kind of attachment, slight though it may be. He felt himself so happy to see Walter, he even felt a momentary impulse to embrace him. At the least, he *did* feel like he should greet

Walter. Thinking about what he had seen in his own journey, he realized with a sense of disbelief what Walter might have had to endure in order to be standing where he currently was.

Then it dawned on him that Walter had arrived before he and the driver had. He marveled that this could be so. He wondered if Walter had passed through the other manifestations with the same ease with which he had the second manifestation, or if indeed Walter had endured the same sufferings the other beings had been seen to endure, albeit with a speed that for some reason was far greater than that in which the others had passed through. He wanted to understand how Walter could possibly have arrived at this manifestation so quickly, and more than that, he felt a sudden compulsion to ask.

It wasn't merely curiosity that drove him, but a sudden sense of awareness of how devoid his journey had been of contact with another being with whom he could relate. The driver offered communication, and even conversation to a degree, but there was no way in which he could really relate to the driver. He didn't know how long it had been since he had expressed *anything* to a being more "on his own level," but he did know that he felt suddenly alone and in need of contact. To communicate anything of his own thoughts and feelings, or for that matter hear those of anyone experiencing anything even vaguely resembling what he was, he was anxious and excited suddenly at the prospect of even possible communication. So, with sudden curiosity in his mind and having had just the slightest hints of aloneness creeping into his heart, his muscles tensed in anticipation of stepping forward to intercept Walter.

No sooner did his muscles tense, however, than did Tim feel a hand rest lightly upon his shoulder, holding him perfectly still to the place in which he stood. "Watch for a moment," came the familiar voice of the driver, calling him out of his emotions and thoughts a bit and into a more alert and clear state of awareness; one without judgments, without the opinions of his mind and gut. He saw the driver's other arm raise and point a finger toward Walter. Walter stopped walking about ten steps or so in front of Tim and the driver.

Walter looked around himself for a moment, seemed to take a very deep breath, and looked at his left arm. Walter then reached over with his right arm, placed his fingers to the edges of a place on his left arm where some skin still remained, and ripped off a fairly large piece of the skin that had still been there. He did this a couple more times, and when he was done the only skin that remained was covering his hand; his fingers.

As Walter had ripped the three large pieces of skin from his arm, a great deal of blood started flowing where he had ripped and fell to the ground below, flowing back toward the circle.

Tim stood in a state of absolute shock, unable to move, or for that matter feel his own body. The sound of the skin ripping off the muscle, Walter screaming, and the blood flowing to the ground had been beyond unbearable. Tim was what most nearly could be described as overjoyed to find that these sounds were quickly replaced by what could only be perceived as the palpitations of his heart beating all the faster with every section of skin Walter removed from his own arm.

The skin Walter removed didn't grow back. The blood merely slowed in the amount in which it flowed down his arm to the ground below over a short passage of time. Meanwhile, Walter looked at his hand, raising it before his face. He cringed and gave a gasp of pain as he managed to create a tear in the skin at the top of his wrist. Then he tore quickly from where the tear was started down to the base of his index finger. He tore the skin up to his finger off its respective bone and muscle, and then continued on. Around his hand he tore skin from muscle, separating the skin of his hand from the skin still remaining on his fingers as he went around the hand. He tore around the base of his thumb, and after letting out a pained gasp, prepared to tear again. He took a deep breath and pulled upward, hard, from the lower left-hand base of his palm toward the tips of his fingers. As he pulled upward, the skin was ripped off the bottom of his hand and straight up to the upper right-hand tip of his pinky, the skin having come off from the underside of his fingers. Walter let out a horrible scream, falling to his right knee as blood flowed from his palm and fingers to the floor. He stood up. He ripped the skin at the top of his pinky back down to the pinky's base and continued around. In two more quick tugs, accompanied by incredible screams of anguish, Walter had removed the skin from his hand. The only skin remaining on his left arm was on his hand, it was the skin on the fingers of the backside of his hand, skin he had been very careful to rip around. Walter looked at the piece of skin he held in his right hand for a brief moment. The palm-side skin of his fingers was the only indication remaining of where this piece of skin had previously belonged, and the fingers hung in a morbidly unnatural manner. Walter dropped the skin to the ground. He then returned to his left hand, ripping the skin from his fingers one by one.

As Tim, much against his own wishes, saw the tearing of skin from each individual finger, he also heard a short scream accompany the ripping of skin from the remaining flesh and bone. As if these sounds were not enough, as the skin from the top of each finger was ripped off, the nail came off with the skin, making an almost imperceptible little "pop" Tim wished had been completely inaudible.

Tim stood frozen, completely aghast. He didn't want to look, but he found himself unable to move, frozen stiff with his horror head to toe. He did twitch a little bit, but it was completely involuntary, and at the time his twitching didn't register in his thoughts as much as his desire to be anywhere but where he was currently standing. He found himself thinking that he would gladly eat worms if it meant not having to watch what was taking place in front of his eyes now. At the moment, however, there seemed to be little he could do about changing the situation in which he found himself; especially since he seemed to have suddenly forgotten how to control the motor functions of his body.

After ripping the skin and nail off the top of his thumb, Walter paused for a moment. His entire upper left appendage was now completely devoid of skin. The blood wasn't flowing at all anymore from most of his upper arm, and the full muscle structure was more or less completely visible now aside from slight trickles of blood that hadn't yet ceased. The blood still flowed rather quickly from his hand, but that too was beginning to slow, and only the backsides of his fingers were particularly bloody.

Walter tossed the small strip of skin pinched between his fingers, formally the top of his thumb, to the ground. He stared at where the strip of skin landed for a moment, took three very long, very deep breaths, and looked to his right arm.

Tim didn't like where this seemed to be going. He had never quite known the kind of sheer horror from which he currently felt himself still completely paralyzed after having seen what Walter had done to his left arm, and did not relish seeing such a thing again. Unfortunately, by the heart-pounding second, this seemed to be exactly what he was in for.

Not unexpectedly, Walter did indeed reach out his left hand, now all bone and muscle and cartilage, and felt for a place on his right arm where skin met muscle so that he could as easily as possible start ripping the skin up and off of his right arm.

The right arm didn't seem as easy for Walter as the left arm had been. There was far more to remove on the right arm than there had been on the left, and while the left arm's skin was separated in almost island-like sections, the skin on his right arm was almost all in one piece. The blood still flowing from Walter's left hand also seemed to add an extra dimension of difficulty in fully grasping his other arm's outer layer. Tim watched, still unable to move, to look away, as Walter tugged and clawed at the skin on his right arm. Walter's yells of pain were stronger than they had been before. Many a violent pull and rip brought Walter to his knees, the pain apparently enough to set him a bit off balance. Blood flowed in mighty streams from his arm to the ground. He seemed to lose composure with every tug to his skin, but he also seemed to work even harder at the task at hand as a result.

As Walter was about halfway through with his upper arm, Tim became aware that the gold around Walter's stomach area seemed a bit lighter than it had been before he started ripping the skin off his left arm. He also noticed that the gold seemed to take on a strange new glow.

Walter continued ripping, and Tim continued watching. The right arm seemed to take a little longer than the left arm had. Though he still felt sickened by the sight he was witnessing, and though every second felt to him lately like an eternity while watching Walter, Tim almost felt as though he was beginning to grow accustomed to the sight before him. Though still wishing he had the ability to vomit, as Walter pulled the last strip of skin off of his upper-right appendage, the skin, accompanied by a nail and an almost inaudible "pop" off the back of his pinky finger, Tim felt that in the near future relaxation might almost be plausible, and for that matter, movement. As this last thought passed across his mind, the skin from the back of Walter's right pinky hit the ground. He watched as Walter took another deep breath, then, as he exhaled, immediately began to claw at the exposed edges of skin around his neck.

Tim's thoughts suddenly froze as a new grip of terror seized any ease left in him and ripped it utterly away.

Walter felt all about his neck for where the skin and the muscle met and tore relentlessly as blood began spurting from his neck and oozing down his upper body. He made rather quick work of his neck skin, and as he started to rip up the skin around the very top of his chest, a natural division between the two sides of his torso seemed to appear. He worked this tear down a little, creating something of a bloody and bleeding "V" of muscle at the very top of his upper chest. Walter grabbed one of the flaps of skin that made up half of this "V" in his right hand and the other flap in his left. He looked down for a moment and breathed heavily.

Tim felt distanced from existence, though paradoxically, still perceiving what was taking place before his eyes.

Apparently with all his strength, Walter pulled his arms, and for that matter hands, downward and in opposite directions. He let forth a scream the likes of which Tim had never heard as he fell to his knees; agony and tears streaming from his face and blood streaming from his chest. He knelt there whimpering in his own blood for several seconds, his hands in the bloody dirt, practically mud, surrounding him. Two pieces of skin that formerly were secured to his upper body now hung at his sides, attached on either side very close to where he might have had a belly button, had he in fact at the moment still had his belly button. He had managed with one mighty tug to rip the skin down his chest and around the void where his belly should have been. The two flaps of skin that had just a moment ago hid Walter's pectoral muscles now no longer hid them. These two flaps hung lazily, resting lightly against his thighs and the ground, curled over in such a way that a nipple could be seen on either side, almost like eyes, creating the appearance of a very large face around where he knelt; the muddy ground as this face's hungry blood-soaked lips.

Tim was –

Walter seemed to struggle ever so slightly to make his skinless arms work for him. He pushed himself more upright, rising to one knee. He then pushed up with his leg. As his second foot found its balance and he found himself able to regain his former standing position, his face flinched with pain as he found himself fully upright. Blood now gushed like a fountain from his upper body. The shade of gold around his stomach wasn't half the brightness it had formerly been, that is, what of that color could be seen behind the micro-sized blood-falls currently cascading over it.

Walter grabbed the large flap of skin hanging from his right side, and with a loud yell ripped the skin halfway down the right side of his thigh. Bending downward to accommodate the fulfillment of his intended action, he ripped down hard again and the skin was separated from most of the outermost side of his lower calf. Walter, now squatting toward his right foot, yanked a third time, and the skin was removed down to the top of his foot. He ripped hard one last time and the skin was completely gone from the right side of his torso, the right half of his right thigh, the right half of his right calf, and the right edge of his foot, all the way down to the heel next to his pinky toe. With tiredness and another facial expression of anguish, he ripped the large pelt of skin from the topside of his pinky toe to the bottom of his heel, and off his body.

Technically, Tim perceived all that was happening in front of him. What he saw registered somewhere within his eyes, other senses, and whatever place they deposited information. However, he was at the moment the perfect embodiment of terrified. Simply being in, or more accurately, *as*, the emotion, as though he, as terror, stood solid and frozen like a block of marble or ice, perception was present. Cognizance, however, was another matter entirely.

The blood flowing from Walter's torso was now reduced to a slow gush; from the right side of his right leg and foot, however, blood continued to flow freely. After tossing the skin from the right side of his body to the ground, he performed almost the exact same procedure on the left side of his body. He now stood with no skin whatsoever from his waist up, at least on the front side of his body, as Tim couldn't see his back, save for the skin that remained perfectly intact on his face. He was also lacking half of the skin from either thigh, as well as a good strip from the left and right sides of his calves and feet respectively. While the bleeding had now all but ceased from his upper body, his legs still bled in copious amounts.

Without hesitating, he began removing the skin under the place his belly should have been. Slowly, and with quick little tugs, he ripped his skin down progressively toward the area of his groin.

When he had the skin ripped down to about half an inch from the base of his penis, he ripped the flap of skin once above his right thigh and once above his left, grunting with each rip and tear. He created a fairly large flap of skin at the top of the remaining skin on his left inner thigh, grabbed the flap, and as hard as he could pulled, releasing a cry of great pain in the process. He panted briefly, then rolled up the skin where it was still attached above his knee, and again with all his might pulled downward, again letting out a deafening scream as he bent himself toward the ground receiving his blood. A third time he pulled and ripped the skin from halfway down his calf to the base of his foot. Walter then ripped the leg skin away from the base of his foot before slowly straightening himself once more from where he squatted in blood-made mud.

He continued onto his right inner thigh, again grabbing the flap of skin with both hands, again tearing his skin from the muscle to which it was attached as hard as he possibly could. This time, he was only able to separate the skin from the top half of his thigh with the first pull. A second pull with all his being, however, separated the skin down to his knee. Three more heartfelt pulls, accompanied by the appropriate screams, shrieks, and grunts of agony, any of which easily with the power to deafen, not to mention the various bows made toward the pools of his own blood forming around him, and a great section of still-bloody skin lay still on the ground beside the inside of the foot it was formerly fully attached to. Walter gave a final rip, and the only covering remaining on either of his legs was the copious amounts of blood flowing freely to the floor.

He finished rolling the remnants of skin previously attached to his right leg, and tossed it aside. He then began removing the remaining skin from his feet.

No skin remained on the outermost edges of the sides of Walter's feet. He sat down in the bloody mud in which he had been standing in order to get into a better position for fully removing the skin of his feet. He scratched at the top of his right foot with the bony tips of his muscled fingers until the top of the skin of his foot started to separate from the muscle beneath it. When he had separated enough skin, he dug his thumb under the small flap and gave a quick, slight rip, wincing as he did. He now got a stronger grip on the expanded flap of skin and pulled quickly and hard once again. The skin on the top of his right foot had now been separated almost all the way up to the base of his toes. He tugged at the skin two more times, and the top of his right foot was fully exposed as toe nails went flying, having popped off the same way his hands' nails had, only this time amplified by five. The skin Walter had pulled off his right foot held on now only at the tips of his toes.

Walter shifted the position he sat in and began to scratch at the back of his right foot by the top of his ankle. He created a little flap for himself and tugged in several short intervals. The blood flowing over his foot made his hands very slippery, and he seemed to have trouble keeping hold of the skin. He also seemed very tired now. He managed to rip up enough skin to get a good grip on the skin attached to the sole of his foot, and was finally able to give the skin a good tug, ripping it up from the bottom half of his foot in the process. Another strong pull, and Walter had ripped up the skin from the undersides of his toes. A final good yank and the skin that had been on his right foot hung freely in the air, being held up to inspection. The two sides of the skin looked odd hanging toe to toe as though gazing at each other for the first time, two parts of the same being from opposite ends of the world. Walter tossed this section of skin aside and began on the other foot immediately.

With several similar quick tugs and rips, his left foot was as skinless as, and bloodier than, his right; by this point the flow of blood from his right foot had slowed significantly. The skin from his left foot was flung to about where the skin from the other foot had landed.

Walter took his time getting back to his feet; the ground had become all the more slippery as blood flowed freely from where his lowermost skin had been. As he again stood full and tall before Tim and the driver, he was now almost completely skinless. From the unfortunate point of view Tim had of the front side of his body, he took in the full picture. Walter was now a figure comprised entirely of muscle and bone with a couple of small exceptions; his facial skin was still completely intact, and the skin surrounding his groin still remained whole as well. Aside from these two lone islands of skin still fixed to the front of his body, the gold that before had been almost opaque over his stomach and shoulders was now practically completely transparent. Only a hint of gold remained, yet somehow with a greater glow than had been present before.

Walter stood fairly still for a good minute. He breathed fairly heavily and looked like he was trying to recover strength. After taking a brief rest, and apparently taking stock of himself, he looked down to the sole patch of skin still clinging to his lower body. Slowly, he began picking at the top of the skin under his belly with his thumbs. When he had something of a flap to hold onto, he started making very tiny, very quick little tugs.

Tim was still taking in stimulus, he still perceived, but he watched now from a place of silence. As far as he was concerned, his body, his mind, these things which he had always previously thought of as perfectly obedient parts of the being that he was that he had considered for the most part under some form of control he called "me," were now the narrow box and window out of which he witnessed the happenings of the Heaven around him from a place of complete and perfect silence. Although the sound of every bloodcurdling scream of pain, agony, and anguish, every minute wrenching of skin from its hold to muscle, every drop of blood hitting the ground and flowing slowly back to the circle to stoke the red flames of this Heaven registered in his ears, he heard it all so clearly because he experienced it directly juxtaposed to the silence he found himself completely immersed in. Sound became the sight of one's finger moving when one's hand is numb. He perceived all that was before him, but not through emotions, mind, or body.

Walter had separated his skin from its muscle down to the base of his penis. He took in a very deep breath and grabbed hold of the skin tightly with both hands. Deep concentration forming on his brow, and apparently with all the will he could draw forth from himself, as he pulled downward with all his strength he simultaneously let out with his breath a great scream of incomprehensible agony.

Tim watched from a place of silence in his mind's eye as though shriveled in the corner of a room and looking out a window at the other end, only because he could not find a way to pry away his gaze. This perspective as it was, his sight intercepted a single teardrop from the corner of one of Walter's eyes.

Walter paused for a moment. He held his genitalia in his hand, just looking at it. A small tube of bloody cartilage showed on the top of his penis where the skin had been torn away. The several small layers of skin still meekly holding on to the bottom of his penis were supported at the moment by his hand.

After several seconds of just staring, he moved again, quickly. He started working around the bloody cylinder still attached to the underside of the penis, still attached to skin. He made a series of what appeared to be hundreds of tiny little tugs, working the skin off the small bloody tube it clenched so tightly to. He winced in pain with every small movement he made.

After a minute or two of this, he was able with one good, strong yank to remove the skin from his penis straight down to the scrotum. He then took another very deep breath, and while pulling hard at the skin previously attached to his penis with his right hand, with his left hand he pushed up on the bottom of his scrotum. He hooked his left thumb under the opening now created at the top of his scrotum and swiftly pushed out his testicles. He grabbed hold of the remaining skin with his left hand, and with one apparently incredibly difficult and concentrated jerk, one scream that surpassed anything Tim had ever heard prior, and a minor flood of blood pouring forth from the area of his genitalia, he had managed to extricate from himself almost every square millimeter of skin on the front of his body. The only skin that could be seen from where Tim's body stood, almost as though waiting for its driver to return, was the skin that made up his face still holding resolutely to the muscle beneath. After the last hard pull of skin from body, Walter's face was as stone.

Walter threw the small, shriveled piece of skin in his hand to where the rest of his skin lay. He reached behind him and quickly plucked several small pieces of skin from his back, buttocks, and the back of his legs. He also tossed these minor strips of external-most flesh to where the rest of his no longer necessary covering had come to rest.

For the first time since Walter had begun removing his skin, Tim felt some semblance of warmth pass through him and briefly recalled his body as though from a great distance in a dream.

For a long moment Walter looked at Tim. His gaze seemed to pass straight through Tim's countenance, confusion of emotion, and stagnation of thought. He seemed to look actually *at . . . Tim.*

There was something gentle in Walter's eyes. The irises of his eyes showed large, black pupils filling almost the entirety of the iris in either eye, but there was a band of light gold surrounding the darkness that was almost soothing to Tim. His eyelids hung relaxed, although quite open, and there was something infinitely peaceful and resolved in his gaze. In those empty places on his body where there before had been an intense shade of gold covering, where there had once been more substantial tinting, now only a hint of gold remained. These curvatures in his body now seemed very exposed, but also were somehow still contained by this lingering hint of golden radiance, this glow. In fact, there now seemed to be a light glow over the entirety of his body.

Walter turned his head toward where Tim and the driver had originally entered, and began walking.

Tim stood remaining stock still with his gaze firmly fastened to where Walter had been moments before. As Walter passed by him and the driver, his own gaze fixed fast upon his intention of destination, Tim stayed exactly as he had the past several minutes unflinching. He barely registered, and yet did register, the light touch of the driver's index finger on his left shoulder as his body swung around, his gaze once again returning to Walter's form as his own body turned as though rotated atop a turntable. As his eyes came in contact with Walter's back, they were able to see that it was completely skinless; they continued to watch as muscle vanished into the clouds of red that drifted between the current manifestation and the main road. He stood remaining transfixed, and the driver stood beside him.

"Most, Tim," the driver spoke in a very light, very soothing tone as he put the rest of his hand slowly to Tim's shoulder, "wait inside the circle for a very long time for their skins to be removed by these beings of divinity. Indeed, eventually, if given enough time, every being here *will* lose that outermost layer of their perceived beings, thereafter passing on. It can take a very long time, though.

"You saw yourself how fast the skin grows back on these inside the circle who are so reluctant to losing that part of themselves they perceive as being so important. It can take a being many times longer to resign themselves to the loss of their skin than it ever took to accept the taste of worms and the loss of a stomach. It varies, though, from being to being."

Tim was aware of the hand on his shoulder, even though he could not yet feel it per se. He was, however, just barely, able to detect the presence of his own blood, much like one would barely perceive the trickle of a small brook from the other side of a large forest. Whereas before, when Walter had looked *at* him, he was able to recall having once had the capacity to remember warmth, now he was almost able to detect the slightest hint of warmth in his own body.

"Some are stripped of their skin almost immediately after entering by those beautiful beings of divinity. Some it takes eons before they begin to release their reservations about what must come to pass before they can proceed.

"Some, however, have a greater instinct, a sort of pull to move forward. That draw may be so great, in fact, that they might take the burden upon themselves to make the changes to their self-conception necessary in order to move forward as expeditiously as possible. This was the case with Walter.

"Walter is a being far more resolute than the vast majority of those making the great trek through the depths of Heaven. We will not see any with such momentum again for many generations. Having even a crude knowledge of the direction he is to take, and learning quickly what is required to move forward, he has shown an incredible determination in processing himself through the manifestations as he has encountered them. Having an inherent understanding of this manifestation shortly after arrival, he allowed what was difficult for him to remove from himself to be removed. After this back skin was for the most part gone, he decided that moving beyond this manifestation as quickly as possible was worth the pain involved in completing the job himself, ripping away his own skin in entirety. Though you can perceive only a hint of the reality before you, can you imagine, Tim, tearing off every inch of your own skin in order to accomplish what you feel to be your very heart's desire?"

As the driver said this, Tim felt that his body must be shuddering. It wasn't a particularly strong feeling, it wasn't a particularly pleasant one either, but it was at least *something*.

"So, though it is rare, on occasion a being will actually alter one's own residual echo of self-conception so severely that they might best continue on their journey toward the fulfillment of what essentially amounts to a really big 'hunch.'" Having said this, the driver swung Tim back around to where his focus had resided before he was turned to watch Walter leave.

Tim remained paralyzed by the sight he had just witnessed for quite some time. The look Walter had given him had, at least to some degree, called him back to the ability to perceive perception, but it took significant time to recall even the slightest recollection of how to utilize the motor functions he had previously been accustomed to. The driver's touch soothed him, however, and helped to slowly bring him back to himself. Nonetheless, even after the driver had concluded speaking, it felt as though hours passed by before he suddenly had reacquired the ability to blink, once.

Ever so slowly, warmth crept back into his core as he continued to gaze forward at the pit filled with whippings and lashings and bitings and cuttings and strippings taking place in the circle before him. The pounding of the drums began to be discerned as an individual sound attributable to hearing as the methodical beat resonated within his ears without cessation. As he began to register that his eyes were seeing, his focus began to expand from pinpointing a single person whipped in the center of the ring to a group of beings being flogged, whipped, scratched, knifed, and beaten; his perspective continued to expand. As the mild heat continued trickling into his blood, the faint smell of strange smokes combined with a crisp, rusty aroma wafted just under his nose. As minutely as these smells began to register did a faint bittersweet begin to creep, slowly, back toward his tongue. As his field of vision extended in front of him, he perceived a rhythmic dance between the beating of the drums and the lashings of the various instruments, followed closely by wails and screams, creating almost a sort of grotesque symphony. The lowering of hands coincided with the resounding beats, and the floor ran alive with blood flowing to the outer edges of the circle, gushing forward in minute waves. Flames around the circle flickered, casting dancing shadows over those whipped, those whipping, those beating drums, the walls, and the flow of blood across the ground. Tim's vision widened until all of these things vibrated together before him in a single breadth of sight.

Then, these disparate features began to blend into each other. The shadows swirled around the fire. The tables and stones and legs of those in the circle bled into the flow that reached up to their ankles. The downward and forward moving lashings and flashes of fire and shadow were becoming indistinguishable from each other. Sounds of flowing and pumping and cracking and crashing and lashing and gashing and gushing and thumping and pounding and thumping and pounding and thumping and pounding, and Tim's vision became one massive, dripping, pulsating unit beating loudly in dark purples along the edges and deep reds in the center, with flecks of orange and all shades in between. A large mass pumping and beating and flowing as though one before his eyes and within his ears; and the rhythm filled him as he became aware of this image's lesser cousin coinciding rhythmically in response in the recesses of his chest, mumbling meekly, but becoming slightly stronger subsequently by the beat.

Then, his eyes blinked a second time.

His vision expanded outward again to reveal its individual parts. He was awestruck by his sudden resurgence of perception and the way it manifested; though he still was not particularly predisposed to movement, he was now fully aware of the feeling of the warmth of the driver's hand on his shoulder.

"It's time for us to move on now," said the driver. "Don't worry about *trying* to move. Your body will know what to do as you return to what you more generally refer to as your 'self.'"

The driver took his hand from Tim's shoulder and repositioned it within Tim's hand. Just as the driver had said, his hand gripped the driver's with no particularly conscious impulse on his part. With a slight tug from the driver, his feet followed in full obedience without the need for explicit instruction.

As they turned to leave, he noticed between where he stood and the red clouds from which they originally entered, several dozen forms sitting in what looked as ever to be deep meditation.

"There were more of them in the fourth manifestation too," remarked the driver, "mostly on the other sides of the doors. We were moving a little quickly for you to pinpoint much beyond the obvious, and in the fourth manifestation they tend to be spread a bit thinner than in other manifestations."

Tim thought he recognized a handful of those sitting in front of the clouds from previous manifestations. A couple of bald monks, a heavily bearded man, and a pregnant woman all struck a chord of familiarity and recollection in him. Noticing them a little bit longer, he had the strong sensation that almost all of them seemed at least a little familiar.

These feelings, along with other perceptions of his surroundings, drifted slowly in and through his head as he and the driver passed once again through the red mists.

Within the driver's reassuring grasp, he stepped lightly over the water of the middle path without a thought and was easily escorted back to his seat. He sat in relative silence and serenity as the driver took his seat. The doors of the bus closed, and the familiar vibration of the engine turning over was felt under posterior and toe.

Book 8
Things Heat Up

The bus continued down the golden road. Without much movement, Tim stared forward fixedly, now able to perceive, though not yet ready to interpret consciously, the data taken in by his senses. He saw that there was a difference between the torches and the walls, but that was a matter of names. Caught between recollections of the entire journey, trying to make sense out of what he most recently witnessed, and a slowly growing strand of gratitude for no longer being completely numb, he didn't care about concerning himself with names at the moment. He enjoyed having found an entirely new appreciation for the simplicity of his surroundings; he was content to sit for a while. And he sat, and time passed.

He did not initially perceive a passage of time. He sat in his state of rest and veritable tranquility and thought not at all of torch after torch illuminating grayish-brown cave, and he certainly didn't consider the length of time he sat in this state. The bus rolled on, the torchlight shined into his eyes, and the texture in the rock was illuminated before him, but there was no thought of conception. There wasn't really any thought at all.

There was sight of light and perceived variation in surface consistency. There was a soft resonate hum of distant sounds colliding in on subtle omnipresent buzz. There was a subtle fragrance just beyond certainty. There was warmth slowly filling his body while his heartbeat grew fainter, merging with the cadence subtly noted by his other senses. In this way, slowly, ever so slowly, he perceived the "world" moving around him until such time as he began to learn again how to consciously direct his perception toward specific detail.

Torch after torch passed before his eyes, and he began to cognize that torches were passing by him. Slowly, the thought arose that what he was passing through was a very long tunnel, a cave, and that torches were illuminating this cave. He identified to himself the driver and the bus. He identified himself *in* the bus. The warmth that he felt within him, and surrounding him, slowly grew in intensity as he had these thoughts and began once again to identify.

He felt the warmth slowly grow, and he continued to watch the torches. He liked that he knew that these were torches, and that they were passing by him. He watched the trails that the light from the fire made as the bus rolled past each torch. He watched the shapes of the dancing flames and saw the illuminated walls, and the shadows dancing over the illuminated walls, upon the illuminated walls. As the bus rolled on, he felt warmth.

He recognized all of the details of the things surrounding him and, one by one, began to recognize their names and apply them accordingly. He became more grateful with each name he was able to attribute to each detail of the world he perceived surrounding him. The warmth around him and through him grew.

He noticed the water. He noticed the gold. He noticed the clouds. He noticed the different way that each torch reflected off the water and the gold and the clouds. He delighted in being able to name all he saw. The warmth increased, and he perceived that he named the warmth increasing.

Tim noticed the bus. He then named every detail he could make out about the bus. He saw the driver, and simultaneously his father; he named as well as he could what he had the impression of seeing. And the heat grew.

Then, he noticed his right hand resting on his left leg. He consciously became aware of his body. He saw his left hand and his left leg. Tim began to perceive as much of himself as possible, and as he did he remembered another body. A naked body he could clearly make out through his mind's eye. He recalled Walter tearing his own skin from his own muscle, slowly, bit by bit. Within the ever-growing heat perceived by him, around him and through him, he perceived a great chill bolt through his spine, through his being. Then he was grateful for the skin that covered him, and he wept, and he held his skin to his skin, and he kissed his skin, and he thanked his skin.

Tim spent many more moments grateful for his own skin as he wept and held himself. When he had done this for some time, he looked up into the reflection in the window of the bus, catching sight of his self in a familiar position. Seeing his reflection but for a moment, he immediately relaxed his muscles and let his body unfurl. The heat increased.

He sat himself up and looked ahead. He saw the paths and the cave and the torches, and, far ahead, darkness. He let himself relax and let his newfound thoughts wander. He thought about his first steps onto the bus and the door snapping shut behind him. He thought about the incredible fear that had gripped him while riding in this bus on the Earth's surface, recalling that he had mistaken that paltry fear for true terror. He then reflected on his encounter with the Gatekeeper and the subsequent manifestations of this place called by the driver "Heaven." He noticed how relaxing the moment was, gazing into the darkness ahead, despite it all. He relaxed and let his self be calm. He let thoughts drift in and out of his head and, regardless of brief flashes of emotion raised from his thoughts, was able to let himself relax after each recollection and consideration. He felt the warmth grow more.

His eyes shut, and he continued to allow himself to fall further into relaxation. Thoughts drifted into a calming void, and he didn't know how long that had taken, and he didn't particularly care. After all he had seen, he was grateful that he could fall into a state that was relaxed at all. Time passed, indicated by nothing more than the heat that continued to grow through him and around him. And the heat grew.

When the heat had grown enough that Tim began to be able to distinguish his state of being as "discomfort," he was quickly brought out of his relaxed trance-like state and his eyes snapped open attentively. The heat was now making him uncomfortable, and he wanted to know why. Looking around, all he saw was the inside of the bus, the driver, the three paths, the torches, the cave walls, and the darkness ahead.

The gradual strengthening of heat brought him back to himself, and it was becoming more and more uncomfortable. He was slowly being made anxious by the heat, but the bus rolled on, and despite his growing apprehension, he tried to remain relaxed. But the heat continued to grow.

At first he noticed that it was merely uncomfortable enough to irritate him to the point that he couldn't let himself relax anymore, but it continued to grow. He continued to try to keep himself calm, but more and more the heat was being felt, and before long, a frantic feeling crept into him almost more quickly than the heat. Slowly, as the heat grew, so too did his dread at what he might see next. His muscles tensed by each passing second as the heat grew stronger. The hotter it became, the more claustrophobic he felt, the more he tensed, the more agitated he got that he didn't know why it kept getting hotter, and exactly what it meant that it did.

While no more than the span of a single full rotation of the long arm of a clock passed that he was in this state, becoming more and more disturbed by each rising fraction of a degree, time felt like it had stopped, as though he may face this torment and torture of ever-rising, skin-melting, suffocating heat forever. Concentrating more and more on his ever-increasing suffering, every second felt like an eternity, and he passed the time in such a way that it felt very much akin to infinity.

To Tim's credit, he *did* remember the words that the driver had repeated many times thus far during his journey, and he did *try* to relax. Unfortunately, the more he tried, the hotter he felt and the more frustrated he became. So, as much as he fought to keep himself calm and relaxed, it just wasn't happening, and he was forced to concede to the tenseness that came so automatically to his body. He allowed himself the severe discomfort of the heat that was ever rising within him and around him. Despite his ultimate inability to relax, however, at no time did he respond to the torture of this heat by curling himself into a fetal ball, though his body seemed to want to move in such a way more and more by the second.

Finally, as the heat grew to a degree that he felt almost completely suffocated and insane, his eyes taking on a crazy wildness that he couldn't do anything about his torment even though he felt with all his being that he must try something, even though there was nothing he could possibly do to avoid the agony of this constantly rising torture; finally, in the distance, while frantically searching everywhere in the hopes that perhaps somewhere was some source of possible relief that he had overlooked, he caught a glimpse of something out of the corner of his eye, and, looking now to the road ahead, which previously had been pitch black, now he could swear that ahead of him lay yet another soft, red glow.

The bus continued down the golden road, the light glow perceived by Tim beginning to grow in intensity as the bus moved apparently closer. The bus rolled on, and the heat grew, and the red glow ahead grew. He became even more anxious now, anticipating what this new ominous red glow in the distance might bode, but having at least *something* to anticipate, he was able to let his self relax, at least ever so slightly.

The bus moved forward. The heat increased. Tim grew tenser. The red glow ahead grew brighter. The bus twisted and turned down along the golden path through the cave. Slowly, the glow ahead filled and illuminated the entirety of the cave.

Tim became more anxious with the mounting heat and its accompanying, brightening glow, desperate to know what was causing the light and the heat and what it would mean. He kept his eyes firmly fixed on the bus's front window, watching the red glow grow and anticipating its source to reveal itself at every turn the bus made.

Many minutes passed with the cave filling with the red glow. Slowly, the red became lighter and lighter as the glow became brighter and brighter. By this time the heat had become truly severe, virtually unbearable. Then, suddenly, as the bus began turning another corner, a light poured down the cave from up ahead, consuming the light of the torches.

As the light flooded into the bus, accompanied by an abrupt, strong wave of heat, Tim saw two large pillars of fire, about 300 feet or so in the distance, rising out of two short, though nonetheless huge, braziers, each standing on three legs, one brazier on each side of the cave. The flame from each brazier rose high into the air, flattening out and finally dissipating after hitting the ceiling of the cave, which stood no less than twenty-seven feet high. Between the flames was a very large circle carved into the cave wall, shaped like a snake devouring itself at the tail. Its head was at the very top of the circle, by the ceiling, and dead center in Tim's field of vision. The snake's fangs were large over its own tail. The snake's eye, even from a distance, seemed to stare straight into the center of Tim's very being. The body of the snake looked almost alive; if not for the brief break at the bottom of the circle where the snake's body seemed to dissolve into the ground under the three paths which crossed over and passed through the giant porthole that was the snake, Tim would not have been certain that what he perceived ahead was nothing more than an intricate stone carving.

The heat was extreme. As the bus rolled slowly toward the colossal snake ahead, Tim, while in some small way relieved that he now perceived the most likely source of the heat slowly lighting microscopic flames one by one in every individual cell of his flesh, was on the other hand still a touch nervous, not knowing what the heat, or for that matter the snake, meant.

Beyond the porthole, the snake, he saw vaguely that the paths looked different. As the bus moved closer to the snake, and his eyes were able to focus more on what lay beyond it, he was able to make out what looked like the paths of gold and cloud beginning to incline upward just after the snake. The path of water, however, seemed to continue down the same horizontal plane it had occupied during the rest of the journey.

Seeing the giant snake eating its own tail reminded him of the archway he had passed under in the third manifestation of Heaven. Thinking that the porthole before him was most likely the dividing point between this and the next manifestation of Heaven, he immediately became much less apprehensive as to the why of his situation. Though this one tension was relieved, the heat was still unbearable and caused him to contract his muscles in such a way that he squirmed in his seat incessantly, if not breaking out into a full writhe, as the bus continued forward. In fact, after considering the probable function that this opening before him served, he recalled the unbearable-- though the word in light of his present situation would have been laughable had he been in any position to laugh, which he currently was not--surge of heat that spread over him the last time he had passed under one of these "signifiers of transition."

126

Recalling the hell-blaze that ran through him as he had passed under the previous archway made him squirm even more with the anguish of anticipation when he considered how much greater the pain he suffered now compared to then already. Try as he might to relax, he was once more developing knot upon knot of tension within.

Looking briefly in the driver's rearview mirror, Tim could swear he saw a large smile on the driver's lips lit up by the two pillars of fire that stood before them. He was suddenly certain of the driver hearing his thoughts, and was put through the further discomfort of not being able to determine the direction of his own thoughts in any way due to the pain. He looked down quickly at the driver, but the driver's face was quite expressionless in the emanations of the blaze in the distance.

200 feet or so from the snake and the fire, he felt as though his skin was fire, so beyond unbearable was the heat that had completely consumed him. He felt as though his blood was coming to a slow boil; as though the heat was closing in on him from all sides; as though the greater the heat increased, the greater he felt in his head as though the heat slowly cooking his body was searching desperately for a release through his skull. Moving closer and closer to the snake by the second, the heat increasing now with ravenous speed, he simultaneously abhorred the thought of any further forward movement, and yet desired nothing but for the bus to reach its top speed so that he might find himself on the other side of the porthole, where he must also find relief from this all-consuming, constricting heat.

Being closer to the other side of the porthole, Tim very clearly saw that while the path of water continued on its course, not only did the other two paths incline upward, but the paths went high enough that they left his range of vision altogether. He also could see that there didn't seem to be supports of any kind under the paths of gold and cloud.

A hundred feet now from the snake, the heat, even though it felt as though it couldn't possibly get any hotter, got hotter. To add further aggravation to his growing plight, while the bus did continue rolling down the path of gold, it seemed to be slowing. While he looked up at the snake, the snake's eye caught hold of his two. Adding a new kind of pain into the heat that he didn't understand how he could feel without being on fire himself to begin with, an unexpected chill added a level of paradox to his suffering. He abruptly felt certain that while the rest of the snake was of stone, its eye was *not*. As this notion crossed through Tim's head, a certain kind of dread fell over him as he found himself suddenly unable to avert his gaze from the snake's single, large, black eye.

It was hypnotic. While the snake's single-eyed stare was penetrating from 300 feet off, now Tim felt as though its gaze had entered the very center of his being, making him completely unable to look away. He felt as though the heat was consuming his flesh inside and out, but now, as he looked deeply into the snake's single, black eye, he felt a new kind of warmth begin to rise in the center of his solar plexus. As he began to feel this new heat begin he could swear he saw the eye change color to a very deep shade of purple.

Seventy feet away, his eyes stayed fastened to the snake's single solid pupil while it became a brighter and brighter shade of indigo. As the snake's eye lightened, so too did the center of Tim's chest feel more and more as though a magnifying glass aiming at his center-most being was rapidly gaining heat from some powerful source of light beyond anything perceptible in the room that surrounded him. The eye seemed bound to him, and he was certainly transfixed by the eye of the snake. The eye became brighter shades of violet with each passing moment until it evolved into continuingly transitioning shades of red; maroon, scarlet, blood.

Fifty feet away from the large, perfect circle that opened in front of the bus, the eye's color moved into ever-lighter reds until transitioning finally into oranges. While all the heat around and through him continued to mount and climb beyond belief, it was the new, quickly rising heat in his center that was truly maddening, and he screamed and squirmed in his chair accordingly. Still, he could not break the gaze of the snake's one eye, transitioning now into yellow. The heat rose while he no longer felt any faculty of control over the movements of his body. He surrendered himself to the whims of his physical form; muscle contractions so severe they now spasmodically contorted his shape as many an ear-piercing scream was let loose without a pause to consider the action.

Twenty-five feet from crossing beyond the carving, the snake's eye was a very light, very bright yellow, and Tim's center convulsed from the pinpoint of heat now cutting deeply into him amidst the Hell-fire sensation he already felt around and throughout the rest of his being. Very close to the snake now, it humbled the bus, towering over both him and the driver, the two pillars of fire standing beside it truly glorious. The bus was closer to crossing over and past the snake by the moment, and while the bus was mere seconds away from being through the porthole, he felt every fraction of a second as though it were forever.

The bus was almost upon the snake, and soon the head of the snake, the eye of the snake, would be beyond his view, necessitating a break between the gaze of the three eyes. The snake's eye turned from a bright yellow into lighter and lighter shades until it was practically white. Then, just before his sight of the eye was lost, it turned a bright white of pure, perfect radiance, and the ever-growing point of heat suddenly exploded within him. As the bus slowly crossed below the snake's head and over the snake's body, he let out a great yell of pure, excruciating agony as all the mounting heat ripped through every cell of his body, and suddenly, for but a brief instant, he felt as though he was composed completely of pure light.

The bus finished crossing completely over and past the snake. Tim found himself standing, arms outstretched, looking before him as the brilliant white that had a moment ago blinded his view darkened slowly and focused to allow him to perceive the slow, upward incline upon which he was now riding. Turning to Tim with a warm smile on his face, the driver uttered the simple words he knew must come eventually. "Welcome to the sixth manifestation of Heaven!"

Book 9
Manifestation 6: Reflecting

The golden road was at a steady upward incline, along with the clouds. Between the two sides of the golden road was a gap of nothingness formed by the absent path of water, becoming more vertically distant by the second. As far as Tim could see, no columns, pillars, or supports of any kind held up the road of gold the bus was traveling upon.

"Thought for sure you'd curl up back there," the driver broke the silence. "Fairly impressed you kept your proverbial cool for as long as you did. You've come a long way, little Timmy!"

"Why was I put through that?" responded Tim, still shaking from what he had felt moments ago rip through his being as he slowly lowered himself to his seat.

"You're on a journey to Hell and a little heat is getting you down, kid?" replied the driver, a smile upon his lips. "It's kind of a purification sort of thing. Look, generally people like you don't see any of this, representative of actuality though it may be. You have no real reason to be here at all, strictly speaking, that is. So, the price you must pay to see Heaven before you arrive in Hell is any discomfort you suffer along the way.

"While for you a source of torment, for those on their journey through Heaven the heat is felt as cleansing and rejuvenating; it prepares them for things to come. The heat relaxes and loosens the last unnecessary particles of that portion of their echo of self-conception you see as skin that they might have missed upon leaving the previous manifestation of Heaven. Aside from eradicating these last remaining particles of being, unnecessary here, too miniscule to be otherwise noticed, the heat also contracts their perception of their current form into becoming a more solid form for the sake of the duration of the use of that form, as long as they find it necessary. It also tends to stop the very last of any not meant to continue through Heaven. Of course, aside from any on a journey the likes of which you are currently engaged, it's not often that one makes it so far before being sent elsewhere. It has happened a couple of times, but none has made it further before being turned back. And in your case, a few moments of subtle heat is a small price to pay to ride the path through Heaven. Consider it a necessary inconvenience."

Despite the driver's words, Tim felt it was odd that for that second, suspended in time, he had felt as though he were made of pure light.

He looked up the road ahead. Gazing through the gap previously filled by the path of water, he saw that they were a good twenty or so feet above the ground and continuing to rise at a steady rate.

The gold road continued to rise upward until it leveled off well above the ground, where the path of water still ran straight and quite alone. While the gold road became parallel with the ground, the path of clouds continued to rise upward at the same, steady incline. Try as he might, Tim could not see the place above where the path of cloud became parallel with the other two paths, if in fact at any point it did.

"Now, you're going to want to keep your eyes on the ground below, ma' boy. Your best view will be from the left side of the bus."

Having a sudden flash of recollection about what he saw in the last manifestation, Tim wasn't sure at all that he wanted to see what was below, but he was kind of curious to see what sort of Hell this slice of Heaven might be, and he knew that there couldn't be much skin removal after the previous manifestation. He walked over to the other side of the bus and knelt down on the cushions of a couple of the seats behind the driver. He looked out the window and down to the ground.

He faintly saw the path of water dully illuminated by small sparks of light, apparently the torches on the cave walls illuminating the path below. The path of water appeared naked without the accompaniment of the other two paths. After a minute or so of watching the lonely stream, the cave walls around the path of water began to expand outward. The bus rolled very slowly down the road of gold, and as it did, the cave walls were moving farther and farther apart from each other until, finally, they veered away from each other in completely opposite directions. The large expanse of space created by the absence of walls was apparently filled in all directions by some kind of maze.

Shortly after the point in which the cave walls veered away from each other, there seemed to be some kind of wall constructed. In the middle of this wall was a small opening exactly big enough for the path of water to pass through. After this wall, for what seemed to be miles and miles ahead as well as miles to the left and to the right, the path of water flowed into an incredible maze that seemed to be made up of walls that were all mirrors. Spread out in every direction, apparently without end, was this giant maze of mirrors, and through its entirety the path of water apparently flowed, filling all the space between the mirrors. The closeness of the mirrors on either side was exactly the width of the path of water, no more, no less.

In this maze Tim saw several people walking, each skinless, and each emitting a light golden glow. He saw these glowing, skinless beings wandering through the maze of mirrors, apparently searching for the best path through a minor universe of reflective infinity. He saw also several small figures sitting in several corners of the maze atop the water with their legs crossed in the lotus position. He even saw some of these figures sitting atop the walls of the very thin mirrors in various places where mirrors met to form corners and crosses. He was certain that had he been just a slight bit closer to the ground below, he would have been able to clearly recognize many of these meditating. As it was, he could swear that even from as high as he was, he could recognize some of them anyway.

As he watched the skinless beings walking, seemingly aimlessly through this mammoth maze of mirrors stretched out below him, he noticed that while this entire area of the cave was filled with enough light to easily see by, there didn't seem to be any torches nor any other discernable source of light shedding illumination over this particular manifestation of Heaven. After spending a short period of time observing the way the manifestation was lit, seeing no other explanation, his best guess was that the light cast on the maze must be coming from somewhere under the golden path on which the bus was traveling. Looking briefly in front of the bus, he could see that between the two sides of the path of gold, indeed there did seem to be a great deal of light manifesting and pouring forth.

He looked once more out the side window next to him and continued watching the skinless, stomach-less, shoulder-less, glowing, haloed beings walking through the maze of mirrors. Fairly close to the beginning of the maze, he thought he recognized one of the beings and asked out loud immediately as the thought entered his head with some degree of amazement, "Is that Walter?"

"Yes," answered the driver. "He's been gifted with a predisposition to pass through Heaven at a comparatively rapid rate. It will take him some time to pass out of this manifestation, however."

Tim watched Walter wander through the maze of mirrors, occasionally walking into a solid wall or two as he tried to make his way through, for as long as he could as the bus rolled slowly along above the maze.

When Walter was finally out of his range of vision, he began watching other beings wandering through the maze. He noted the similarity of their movements in relation to the movements he had noticed Walter making. All in all, the images he saw were very consistent, since there were few variations possible to walking around, and occasionally into, the mirrors of the maze. Looking as far as he could forward, he saw no end to the maze in sight; no place where the road of gold seemed to drop away and begin to descend again. He wondered how long it must take for a person to find their way through to the other side.

A great deal of time passed, perhaps forty-two minutes, that he watched the maze of mirrors and those walking through it and meditating in and on top of it. Aside from a couple of instances in which a glowing being materialized out of "nowhere," monotony was consistently firmly formed. He looked up and forward, and saw that the end of the maze still seemed nowhere in sight. He was about to ask the driver exactly how big the maze was when the driver cut off his thought. "Keep looking, Tim. Look at that, what you would identify as a woman, walking down over there in the distance. Watch her."

Indeed, Tim saw a woman walking a bit of a ways in front of his more immediate field of vision. He saw no other beings close to where she walked. He began watching her as she moved; only being able to tell she was a her because of the odd clumps of what seemed fatty and veiny on her chest, her lack of anything where even a small bit of something had continued to cling onto Walter in the way of genitalia, and her face, which even at a distance was eerily pretty and stuck out as a lone island of skin against a body otherwise almost completely covered in muscle. The bus continued to slowly roll forward.

He watched this woman intently as she wandered through the maze. There didn't seem to be anything particularly unique about this woman. Just like the others in the maze, she wandered around apparently aimlessly and apparently quite some distance from the maze's end. And, just like the others, she not too infrequently found herself walking into mirrored walls, apparently mistaking certain mirrors at certain angles for a new turn that might bring her closer to an end to her confused wanderings.

The bus was just about aligned with where the woman was walking, and the woman had just come to the end of a particularly long, straight corridor of mirrors leading her no closer to the finish of the maze, and in fact a dead end, when the bus stopped.

Tim continued watching the woman. She was now staring at herself in the mirror at the very end of the stretch of mirrors she had just wandered down. After studying herself in the mirror for a long minute or two, she suddenly let out, at the top of her lungs and height of her throat, a very loud, very shrill, highly deafening, blood-curdling scream that hit Tim's ears like a bullet before apparently ricocheting back out across the rest of the maze. This was a long scream that lasted some many, many seconds. Once this scream had ended, she screamed again . . . and again . . . and again.

Tim recalled his own behavior in another time and another place as he listened to this woman screaming this way for quite a few minutes. When she had finished screaming at her own image in the mirror, she began to strike both of her muscular hands against the mirror until the mirror cracked into many pieces, slivers, sections, and shards. With one of the bloody mounds of muscle she had used to beat repeatedly upon her own reflection, the woman reached toward a large shard of glass, of mirror, hanging loosely onto the other fractured fragments of mirror, and picked it off from where it hung.

The woman looked at her face for a moment in the mirror to her right. She then turned her head and looked for a moment in the mirror to her left. Finally, she spent a moment looking at her face in the broken mirror in front of her. Tim saw that the place from where she had taken the shard of mirror, now held bloody and tight in her hand, created a sort of void in the reflection over a part of her face.

She raised the shard of glass to her face and began to peel off the last scrap of skin holding still resolutely to the rest of what Tim perceived as being her body. Piece by piece, she took off the skin on her face. Holding the shard of mirror to where the edge of the skin met its muscle, she scraped up the skin and cut it off, letting it drop to the water below where it began to dissolve instantly and sink into oblivion. Then she began again, peeling off the skin of her face, piece by piece, chunk by chunk. Blood flowed freely from where she cut. Blood streamed down her body from her face. Blood covered the hand, and the shard of glass she clung to as she scraped up, off, and severed. Drop by drop, stream by stream, blood flowed to and into the water at her feet; pieces of skin fell down to and into the water at her feet.

Tim watched for several minutes as she passed the shard repeatedly over her face, slicing off bit by bit, slice by slice. Mildly stunned and thoroughly disgusted, he reverted in some degree to the state of catatonic shock he had become accustomed to in the previous manifestation

The woman sliced off ribbons of her face and ripped them off one by one. She cut off chunks of cheek. She placed the shard to the edge of her upper lip and peeled it off, running her muscled thumb over the top of her lip to keep it steady as she ran the shard of bloody mirror under it. She then turned her focus to her lower lip and lopped it off likewise. She held each eyelid taut as she cured herself of blinking, slicing them off one, two, three, four, the upper lids and the lower. She took the shard to the base of her ears, sawing them off left, right. She peeled off pieces of proboscis, that is, the tip of her nose came off with the rest of the skin she worked off with the shard of mirror she held in her hand.

When she was done, no skin remained on her body. Her visage was a mask of blood giving way to muscle as the blood flow slowed. In the end, for all intents and purposes, the woman was faceless.

Having removed her face, the woman looked at the hole in the mirror where she had removed the shard she had used. She reached out to touch the hole, and as she did, the mirror healed itself. What had looked like empty space a moment before became again solid mirror just as the woman's fingers came in contact with the spot where the shard had been. Not only had the hole become again mirror, no longer did a single crack in the mirror remain. It was as though the mirror had never been touched.

Still clutching the bloody shard tightly in her continuously bloody hand, the woman again pounded at the mirror with her fists. This time it did not break. She continued to pound for minutes, running into the mirror with the full force of her body. Again and again she threw her body against the mirror, and with each impact, the mirror betrayed not so much as a tremor or a scratch to indicate that it has been assaulted in any way. The woman stopped, looked at the mirror, and again began to scream just as loud and as long as the last time, perhaps even more so now, apparently from frustration. When at last she stopped, she stood where she stood silently, looking at her own reflection for some time.

Fighting off his initial impulse to fall back into the farthest reaches of his mind where his senses could detach from his immediate consciousness, Tim watched the woman more actively than passively once she had ceased removing her face. As he watched the woman and her reflection in the mirror, though she lacked adequate means of such expression, Tim could swear that he saw her facial muscles contort into something resembling a scowl.

The woman stared in this way for some time while Tim, fairly quickly, began to recover his faculties once again. Judging from the way her chest expanded in and out, the woman was apparently breathing heavily, and she seemed very unsure about what to do.

Tim watched her stand in indecision until, slowly, she stepped up to the mirror and put her free hand onto it. She placed her fingers on the mirror over the reflection of her face. She passed the tips of her fingers lightly over the section of mirror several times as though tenderly touching the face in the mirror, feeling its texture beneath her fingertips. She took a couple of steps backward, looked at herself in the mirror, contracted the muscles around her eyes as though attempting to squint, then contracted the muscles around her eyes as though to open them wide; took a deep breath in, let it back out, and while letting out that breath of air, raised the shard of glass into her left eye socket.

She inserted the mirror shard in toward the bottom of the socket and, using the shard as a lever, popped out her eye and swiftly cut the cord attached, the optic nerve and the eye's muscles, severing her eye from the rest of her body. She let the eye drop, then repeated the procedure with her right eye, screaming a bit as she cut out each eye.

Tim's sense of extreme shock was renewed before the first eye fell to the water below.

The second eye, along with its still attached cord of nerves and muscles, fell beneath the surface of the water as the freshly blind woman took a step forward. As she did so, her eyes reappeared at once.

The instant clenching of the woman's perfect white teeth reflected in the mirror as only a mere moment after the regeneration of her eyes, the woman plunged the sharp end of the shard directly into her right eye repeatedly. Liquid, puss, and blood poured profusely down her face. She dug out every remnant of eye contained in the socket, then continued to shove the point of the shard into her other eye, scraping every bit of matter out of *it*. Finally, she reached into each socket and, with a long scream, ripped out what remained of the optic nerves and the muscles. As she took out, apparently, the last of the remnants of her eyes, the mirror in front of the woman suddenly brightened to gold followed by perfect transparency, revealing an apparent blackness, a void, before shattering into a cascade of seemingly infinite pieces discernable only by the light above they reflected, falling into the water below. As the shards of glass fell below the place the woman's eyes had been, two rays of gold shot into the darkness before her. The woman dropped the bloody, dripping shard to the water beneath her feet, where it sank down to join the rest of the pieces of mirror. The woman walked along the path now open before her, the odd golden light shining from the place her eyes had been into the apparent darkness. As she passed out of sight and into the unknown blackness, a mirror appeared, the section of maze once again as it had been before she had entered it.

While having not sunk to the same sensorial devoid depths of his psyche that he had in the previous manifestation, Tim nonetheless had fallen into a mild form of the same basic paralytic state the second time the woman had begun to gouge out her own two eyes. He had perceived every moment of what had occurred, but not entirely of his own desire to perceive it so much as his inability to move once duly frozen with fear at perceiving what the woman was doing to herself and reflecting, but for a moment, on his own anatomy; namely, his eyes. By the look of him, he wasn't going to be moving any time in the near future.

He heard the light, low sound of the bus's engine turn over. He saw the movement of the maze and felt the slow rolling of the wheels and the gentle vibrations of the engine. He then heard the driver's voice as though slightly distant, but wholly audible in his ear. "Try to remember, dear boy, it's only an indistinct representation of a truth you cannot now possibly, even vaguely begin to fully comprehend."

Unfortunately for Tim, however, the indistinct representation he beheld did not quickly diminish as the bus rolled on. Beyond that place the woman had been were many others, perhaps thousands, in similar positions repeatedly sticking pieces of glass into their eyes; trying to eradicate the things keeping them from moving forward on their paths through Heaven, but with less fervor, less tenacity, and less apparent initiative. One would stick the piece of glass they held into their eye, then wait before sticking it in again, giving the eye ample time to regenerate. One would angle the glass to lever the eyeball out, and then, upon failure, try the same method again. Another would gouge out one eye completely, and then rest, allowing the eye to come back before the second could be taken away. Another broke the shard, apparently *he*, held into several pieces, sticking shard after shard into his eye, then stopping and slowly scraping little pieces of eye out, bit by bit, one bit regenerating before the eye was touched again, then trying again to break the shard up into even smaller pieces, again sticking them one by one into his eyes. Unlike the woman's, however, the mirror that stood before these new eye-scrapers were of a different tint of gold, each closer or farther toward transparency.

The bus rolled on along the path of gold. Tim stayed stock still in the same kneeling position he had been in while he had watched the woman. He now gazed forward as the maze of mirrors slowly went by; half perceiving in a conscious, willful way, though still far from having regained nearly enough consciousness to be able to take control of his greater motor functions adequately to turn his gaze from those continually stabbing themselves in the eyes in various ways, and the many reflections of these beings in the mirrors surrounding them.

Tim sat, or rather knelt, in such a way for many hours just watching the maze and those within go by under the unblinking watch of his eyes. At some point after apparently thousands had passed beneath his scope, the maze became again mostly empty, a lone far-out gouger passing by now and then only rarely. What felt like days had gone by before he felt a slight reflexive movement in his upper arm muscle. He took it as a good sign. As he continued kneeling and watching the maze go by below him, the driver began to talk.

"At this rate, you'll be back to your old self in no time, kid. You seem to be learning how to relax a little, finally. You should be proud of yourself.

"Think of this manifestation as a place of reflection, so to speak. Each being walks through the maze, but solely intent on continuing their journey, and grown accustomed to radically changing their forms as the necessity for passing onward into future manifestations, they don't stop to consider much what their journeys mean, what the result of their journeys has been, and what their journeys may be. Thus, the beings stumble through the maze, not realizing that they are walking around 'mirrors,' and not at all considering their own reflections accompanying them during almost their entire passage through the manifestation. For those who wander through this manifestation, their sole intent is to move past it and into the next. They have not truly stopped to consider themselves, however, and that is what this manifestation is all about.

"Here you perceive as analogous to the truth of the manifestation, which you *cannot* see, mirrors. Very interesting are mirrors, Tim. You know already of the nature of a mirror to reflect, according to curvature and light, exactly what is put in front of it. This singular characteristic is remarkable in and of itself. What is even more remarkable, however, is a fuller consideration of the implications of perfect reflection. To understand what I mean, consider a simple experiment that you may or may not have tried in your own experience of placing two mirrors face to face and perfectly parallel to one another. When two mirrors are aligned perfectly face to face and stand looking at each other, as it were, there may be seen a glimpse of the face of infinity. But the harder one tries to see it, the more one stands in its way, and ultimately, one's own face gets in the way of perceiving fully the infinite. One may say that the purest face of a mirror is infinity, but if that pure face can only be seen by another mirror whose infinite nature is being reflected back to it— well, perhaps you begin to see now with greater capacity what the meaning of a mirror might entail!

"So, it is not merely of jest that I say that this is a place of reflection. The fact of the matter is that not only is this place a place of great reflection, but that this aim is accomplished through the mechanism of infinity, the only 'entity' by whose face one begins to see the truest aspects of one's true self.

"These beings walk through a maze of infinity, a place without end, unable to exit while they are unable to see themselves. Content only with the journey, and not seeing where they are as they continue along their respective paths, they do not notice themselves or the place in which they tread, and thus may spend a very long time wandering through the infinite realm seen here as a very long maze of mirrors. In fact, they may spend, what you would consider, lifetimes, or even longer than ages, before some will notice themselves being surrounded at every turn and angle by themselves. And even after one does begin to notice the mirrors around them, a problem may arise in any of their perceptions as to how to see past their own face and into the infinite.

"Here our chief example is the woman you saw pass beyond the manifestation. Unlike Walter, she has not been so expeditious in diminishing her echo of self-conception. Distinct from Walter, however, after the great amount of effort it's taken her to 'alter her form' to the degree that she may arrive at *this* manifestation, this manifestation she did pass through rather expeditiously. The same will not be able to be said for Walter, nor obviously for those who you have seen after you saw *her*. It seems both he and them will spend quite a bit of time 'reflecting' before any of these will be inclined to move forward.

"Finally perceiving herself in the infinite, and letting herself perceive in truth what she is, initially that truth was of no comfort to her, and even a great shock after so much time spent caring much less about what she is than where she is going. Stopping to see her self, therefore, caused an initial degree of discomfort she had to work through before being able to continue on.

"If you recall, she had so much dis-ease by the fact of herself that she had to cause a break of her pure perception of who she was in infinity, in order to fully process her own being as it was reflected to her in the clear reflection of forever. It was only then that she began to understand why she walks the path she does, and what she needed to do to continue on her journey through Heaven.

"Seeing her residual echo of self-conception for what it was, seeing the difference between those parts of her that were altered and those that were not, seeing the necessity of changing her form as she had in order to progress through Heaven, she took it upon herself to further alter her own form in order to move beyond. In this case, it was her identity with which she had to part in order to move forward. It wasn't until seeing the void in the mirror, once she picked the piece out of the mirror, that she could understand that beyond infinity there was nothing, and that until coming to nothing, she would not be able to pass beyond the infinite.

"By stripping herself of her own identity, in this case seen as a face, she strove to alter her form so that she could continue onward. But identity is more than merely a mask by which distinguishing features of an individual are separated from the whole. Along with internal identification, identifying oneself as a separate being, one also externally identifies, identification of *other* beings. To move beyond this manifestation, it is not enough to lose internal identification. One must also lose external identification. Seeing again where she stood in relation to infinity, once demolishing the part of her echo of self-perception that was her internal identity, and seeing that she still perceived the infinite, she began to realize what realizing the nothingness beyond infinity truly entails.

"She has never been quick to change her form, but her will to move forward has been always as iron. Hence, in this place, she has excelled in progression where previously she was slow to allow that which was necessary to travel onward. Knowing, finally, that to move into nothing required 'seeing' past infinity, she attempted to cease her identification with that which is external. Her echo of self-conception was stronger than she gave it credit for, however, and, just as in other manifestations when one is not truly ready to part with an attribute, clinging so strongly to that which one considers to be a part of one's being on which they are reliant and which is *needed*, in this case her attribute of external identification represented to you as eyes, they came back, having not been truly removed. So, realizing this and wanting truly with all her being to move forward with her journey, she mercilessly eradicated that part of her 'person' impeding her progress, utterly and completely, with the true determination she felt to move beyond this manifestation and continue journeying forward.

"Without identity, coming to nothing, within the void, she was able to progress beyond this manifestation and into the next.

"And that being said, as to the others, while their will may not be quite as great as hers, they certainly make strides infinitely more progressive toward passing out of this place than those who came before her."

"Now, all things considered, you seem to be doing pretty well, skipper, but there won't be a barrage of heat to instantly warm you in-transit to the seventh manifestation like there was on the way to the sixth. You're already coming back to yourself pretty rapidly, and you should be shipshape in no time, but best for you to be on top of your game for the home stretch, eh? So, I'll tell you what. The greater part of your journey to you-know-where is behind us at this point, and the thing about infinity is that it's a *very* big place. You let yourself regain full composure at your leisure, and just let yourself relax and enjoy the view of the manifestation for as long as you'd like. When you're ready to delve deeper into Heaven, you just let me know. In the meantime, enjoy yourself. Forever is a very long time, and we have nowhere special to be right now."

Still kneeling, still very still, still feeling fairly gripped by the icy-cold hand of fear, Tim watched as the maze of mirrors passed by. For hours, if not days, he gazed out the window down upon the glowing, skinless beings discovering, as best as he could discern through the frost chilling his mind, where and who they were in all that surrounded them. He saw one individual materialize, from apparent nothing, with no skin upon its face and just one eye in front of a mirror already tinted a light shade of gold. He watched the meditators, who could be seen every so often floating on the water, balancing on the tops of the mirrors, and looking as though they were all apparently considering infinity. He watched the infinite network of mirrors, and the long, straight halls of parallel reflection they created; the paths leading to nowhere, mirrors angled to give a different view of eternity, the paths of variation without end all showing the unchangeable unity of forever, spotted by no cessation of difference and variation. He watched for hours as unconscious motor reflex slowly gave way to his relearning, once again, how to consciously influence something as simple as a slight movement in his right little finger.

He felt his own internal heat strengthen as his body began to respond as he had been previously accustomed. Twenty-three hours or days or weeks or so had passed by the time he could slowly move himself from kneeling to sitting. Another many and he could, at least *briefly*, move any and every muscle upon which he spent a moment or two concentrating. After what must have been at least days or decades had elapsed, though by then it had felt to him as though millennia had past, he was able to move himself back to the other side of the bus where he had originally been accustomed to sitting during the duration of the trip. Having once again learned to use his own body, he let himself relax for a while and reflect on his journey thus far.

Some time later, when he felt as though he had found within himself the peace and calm so rarely to be had throughout his journey, when he felt as though he was in the best possible condition he could be in to face whatever might lie ahead, when he felt there was an interestingly unnerving pointlessness nagging at him for keeping himself on a path that led nowhere and did nothing, feeling almost as though whatever horrors lay ahead must be preferable to an eternity of sitting on a bus and watching line after line and corridor after corridor of mirrors, stopping only every so often to watch some determined individual finish gouging out their own eyes, he let the driver know that he felt ready to move onward.

"You sure, kid? We can keep going for as long as you'd like. You know where you're gonna wind up . . ."

"Yeah, I'm sure," responded Tim meekly and with noticeable uncertainty in his voice.

"You got it, scout," said the driver as he apparently shifted gears.

Shortly after the driver had changed gears, Tim saw a wall, much as there had been at the "beginning" of the maze, erected apparently as an "end" to the maze. Looking between the two sides of the golden road, he saw below him and a little to the left the path of water find a small opening just big enough for it in the middle of the wall. He watched as the left and right walls of the cave came back toward each other, bottlenecking apparently at the correct width for the three paths. The path of water, flowing again on its own through bare ground, looked once more a bit lonely.

Looking up, he saw ahead that there was a trail of clouds coming down at an incline from above, hovering just over the sides of the golden road. He saw also that at the point in which the clouds met the golden road, from where he sat, the golden road looked as though it discontinued. A minute or two later, as the clouds came down beside his window and returned to the position he had previously been accustomed to seeing them, the golden road inclined downward and the bus began its decent. Several minutes later, the golden road and the clouds leveled off, being rejoined by the path of water. After a few more minutes had passed, without turning his head the driver uttered the expectable. "Welcome to the seventh manifestation of Heaven."

Book 10
Manifestation 7: Nothing to Lose One's Head Over

The bus continued down the road another quarter hour or so, by Tim's estimation, before stopping again. As the bus stopped, he saw a back of muscle with a golden-tinted glow disappearing in the clouds to the right. He shuddered at this brief glimpse and suddenly felt hesitation to follow the figure's path into whatever lay beyond the clouds.

The door of the bus opened.

"Come along, boy," said the driver in a fairly upbeat tone. "You won't have much trouble walking out of this one on your own legs, I think. You should find this manifestation far more relaxing than the last." Having spoken, the driver descended the stairs of the bus.

With a lack of enthusiasm and a heavy sigh, he stood up and followed after the driver down the stairs. He saw the driver disappearing into the clouds and followed him, reluctantly. He was refreshed by the cool, moist dampness of cloud on his cheeks as he walked through. His feet were soothed by the cool crispness of the firm dirt on which he stepped. In front of him, he could see the flicker of lights, though otherwise his sight was obscured in the clouds through which he walked.

Coming out on the other side, he was greeted by loud, agonized screams. Looking out before him, he stopped dead in his tracks and let out a loud gasp as his eyes widened and his mouth opened enough to let his heavy breath loose. Taking in all that he saw before him, he took three more *very* slow steps forward so as to be able to watch from beside the driver.

Tim saw a glowing, muscled figure get on top of, and lie down upon, a table approximately twenty feet away from where he watched. Hovering behind the form of muscle was a figure clothed in a robe of white which shown so brightly that it made the torches lining the walls of the perimeter of the room wholly unnecessary. The figure seemed to float, though its robe reached to the ground. It appeared to be no less than seven feet tall and had three pairs of wings on its back. Two sets of the wings fluttered in a pulsating, almost liquid-like, motion. The other set of wings brushed back and forth in like motion, hiding the place where its feet would be, if it happened to have any, and the wings being where they were, Tim was not sure that it did. Atop this many-winged radiant being, where one would expect to see a head, there was what looked like a red bag made out of what appeared to be soft, shiny cloth, like velvet. Raised above the red cloth bag was the figure's long, left arm outstretched to its delicate hand, where it held a sort of very large, bloody cleaver. The cleaver came down hard with a severe "CHOP!" followed by a scream coming from the being on the table as the figure quickly pushed the dismembered toe aside with the cleaver and a loud scraping sound. As the toe fell to the ground a new one appeared instantly where the old one had been. Again the figure raised its left arm, and again "CHOP!" a scream, a scrape, a new toe, and again the process repeated.

In this room there were no less than 1,500 tables with similar beings of muscle surrounded completely by a light, gold glow, rays of light shooting into the air from at least 3,000 empty eye sockets, all lying down with various limbs removed, and being removed, by identically winged beings with red cloth, resembling shiny velvet, bags for heads, bright, luminescent, white robes for bodies, three no less luminescent pairs of wings apparently keeping them afloat, and large, bloody cleavers clutched in their delicate left hands *CHOPPING* down hard to separate various limbs from similar muscled bodies.

The rhythmic chopping of the winged beings' cleavers mixed with the agonized cries of pain accompanying them and flooded into Tim's ears in waves like the rising of a high tide. Tim was put a bit on edge by the red rivers flowing off the various tables like two thousand miniature crimson waterfalls. Streams of blood poured out of open wounds where a limb had been freshly severed. Sometimes a limb reappeared instantaneously, stopping the bleeding. On other occasions a limb would not rematerialize, and a great deal of time would pass before the flow of blood would cease, even though a new limb had already begun to be "worked on." The blood would flow down to the ground, which greedily drank every last drop as though it were a giant, thirsty sponge. A light, thin mist of blood hung humid in the air everywhere Tim looked.

As though the blood weren't enough to predispose Tim to be ill at ease, every limb removed lay in a pile on the ground at the foot of the table, stacking ever higher with each loud CHOP under its respective falls-of-blood. He watched as cleavers came down to remove toes, feet, calves, thighs, fingers, hands, arms, and what remained of the beings' genitalia, both varieties of which were as pitiful little lumps of cartilage and flesh which were distinguished from the cracking, swooshing sounds of the removals of the other body parts with a distinctive pathetic *splurch*. A few beings who consisted of just their torso and their head were being chopped at the neck apparently to have their torsos removed, which landed on the ground with a sickening thud before a new torso would rematerialize attached to the neck.

Though feeling incredibly ill by what he was watching, Tim wondered what would happen to the head once the torso was removed for good.

Tim recognized at this point almost all of the 85-some-odd beings he saw meditating on the ground between the various tables. Several of the beings even seemed to float upon the tips of heaps of limbs, though these were a bit toward the back of this "room" and obscured by the thicker reds of the mist.

After several minutes gazing at the activity spread out before him with substantial queasiness, Tim noticed that when a limb did not regenerate, and the blood finally stopped flowing from a wound, a very thin, luminous-gold dome of light would appear, hugging the place where the limb had formerly been. He noticed that the bigger a limb being removed was, the bigger the dome of light that would cover the place where the limb had been previously attached. Shortly after noticing this, the driver raised his right arm and extended a finger, and Tim watched the table at which the driver had pointed.

The being on the table was one of those who had remaining of its body only its head and its torso. Down came the cleaver, "CHOP!" "SCRAPE!" "THUD!" and only a head remained as a single, quick gush of blood poured out from the neck. Tim saw the golden glow that had surrounded the various missing extremities of the torso rise from the dismembered hunk of body as a formless light and hover over the being's head while the flow of blood ceased. Meanwhile the winged figure at the table's side, floating or otherwise, rearranged its position to the head of the table, where it raised its cleaver and chopped down at the remaining head length-wise, straight down the middle. The two halves of the head came back together immediately, and again the cleaver came down, chopping the head in two. The being with the cleaver continued to chop the head in half for several minutes as brain and blood flew each time from the divide created by the large, blood-tinted blade. The golden light that had been floating around the head, often with the rays of light emitted from the head's eye sockets shining straight through it, finally came to coalesce at the neck, which gave the impression of a golden bulb of light stemming out from the being's neck, fueling the rays of gold shooting out from where its eyes would otherwise have been.

The cleaver came down again vertically in the center of the head, "CHOP!" and this time, the two sides of the head did not rejoin. The cleaver then came down width-wise, "CHOP!" and the head was in four pieces. The cleaver scraped away the lower-right piece of head, and a golden radiance remained on the table where the piece of head had been, regrouping with the rest of the golden light formed at the neck. Tim was made further nauseous as he noticed the more fully exposed bits of brain somewhere within the golden glow around the place the removed piece of muscled skull formerly occupied. The cleaver scraped away the upper-right piece, and the golden glow that remained on the table joined fully the rest of the light, as though half the head had been replaced by this strange luminance. Tim felt disgusted at seeing the cross-section of the head's brain through the light, although there was an interesting effect created between the golden dome forming a translucent almost-half a head, and the other very-definitely half a head projecting rays of light toward the ceiling. The cleaver scraped away the lower remaining piece of the head, and the ray of light that had emitted from the right eye socket receded, as though pulled back through the eye-socket as the quarter of skull was swiped away, to join the rest of the glowing mass now huddled around the last quarter of the head. The cleaver scraped away the last quarter of head, and all that remained was a glowing, golden light moving into itself to form a singular entity. It was as though it were liquid merging with itself, trying to find its most ideal shape.

Finally the light gathered itself together into a perfect sphere of slightly golden radiance that hovered about a foot above the table. The winged being 'stood' upright with its arms, one of which was holding a cleaver in its left hand somewhere under its flowing robe, by its sides as though standing at ready to receive an order. The winged being was perfectly still, save for its wings, which were continuously, gently moving back and forth apparently with restful, slight flutters. The sphere of gold continued to hover for a moment over the table.

The sphere then began to move. It floated lightly over the large pile of recently dismembered limbs, which had previously lain in the place the sphere arose. As the sphere passed over them, they sank into the earth on which they sat. The sphere continued moving, floating between wings and tables and piles of dismembered limbs; weaving past cleavers and meditating forms, and hovered gently and serenely as it slowly made its way toward the clouds hiding the paths that ran through Heaven.

Unhurriedly, after a great deal of slow hovering around and past the various obstacles in its path, the golden sphere of light found its way to the clouds and disappeared into them, all the while the chopping of cleavers and screams of pain and relentless torment never subsiding and always supplying the background music for Tim as he watched the sphere slowly make its way from table to cloud.

"Time to go, slugger," the driver said, giving Tim a light pat on the left shoulder.

Looking up quickly at the driver's face with a touch of disbelief, Tim responded, "But we just got here. Not to complain, but aside from the excruciating desire *not* to be seeing this, I haven't even been frozen straight through to the marrow of my bones with fear. That was it?"

With a wide smile and a chuckle, the driver responded, "You really have come a long way, Tim. Just a short while ago you would not have been so light about perceiving a manifestation of Heaven such as this. You ought to be proud of yourself, though pride does tend to lead elsewhere than here. I'll explain to you, to whatever degree you can comprehend, what you have just perceived while we are in-transit to the next manifestation, but you have seen what you were meant to, and it is time to continue forward."

With that, the driver turned and walked toward the clouds. Tim cast a last glance toward the chopping and screaming and scraping and fluttering, then quickly turned and followed after the driver, whose back at that moment was disappearing into the ethereal barrier.

Tim again felt the light spreckles of mist upon his face, the crispness of the air against his cheeks, and the coolness of the ground beneath his feet as he quickly passed through the clouds. Coming out on the other side, he saw the driver settling into his seat. The golden sphere was a bit ahead of the bus, hovering about five feet over the path of water, and floating forward.

Tim ascended the steps of the bus and took his seat. The door of the bus closed and the wheels of the bus turned forward. All the while he could see the glowing sphere of gold hovering in the distance, apparently following the path of water forward through the tunnel.

"Though no less significant than the other manifestations, Tim," the driver began, "the seventh manifestation of Heaven is fairly straightforward in the role it plays for those on their journey through the great depths of Heaven.

"Having been able to let go of one's sense of identity, both inside and out, a being is ready to begin the process of letting go of that part of their residual echo of self-conception perceived by you as their body, and called for the sake of the most accurate communication possible their 'form.' In other words, in order to move into the furthest, deepest, and most absolute manifestations of Heaven, in this manifestation it is necessary that one loses their still-accustomed form.

"Though still beyond your grasp to see truly, the very simple, metaphorical representation which you perceived is a highly adequate representation of that which is actually taking place. Once loss of total identity is achieved in the previous manifestation, these beings come to this manifestation to have the vast majority of the remains of their echo of self-conception, all those remaining qualities and aspects still attached to their most essential or 'true' self which they allowed themselves to re-embody, originally to be able to reconcile the disparate impulses present within themselves to remain attached to a previous life and to progress to the deepest recesses of Heaven, removed from their most essential self, or true self, or 'soul.' The form these beings took originally to navigate Heaven and to be better oriented, there, is removed so that these beings may finally experience the deepest manifestations of Heaven.

"A being enters the seventh manifestation and, with the assistance of an angel, over 'time' the various aspects of a being's echo of self-conception are virtually entirely removed. What you perceived as the removal of a limb is an angel revealing as greatly as possible the truth of a being to that being, so as to assist the being's attempt to perceive the actuality of an aspect of their echo of self-conception and be able to release it after seeing the reality that that aspect of the being is no longer needed, nor part of one's true self.

"As these various aspects of one's echo of self-conception are slowly distinguished and removed from one's most essential or true self, the essential part of the being separates from the part of one's echo removed and reintegrates with the rest of the essential element still utilizing the supposed necessity of an aspect of echo of self-conception for continuing onward. You perceived this as the gold light rising and reforming with the rest of the gold light attached to that which was left on the table, once one of the parts of the being's body had been removed.

"The various aspects of one's form are continually worked on and removed in this way until, in the end, just short of one hundred percent of the being's residual echo of self-conception has been removed and its essence is almost all that remains. In this case a gold sphere, like the one we follow behind now, is representative of a being that is primarily essence and properly prepared for entering the eighth manifestation of Heaven. You see this being in the appearance of a sphere so that you may begin to understand that while formless, even though they now lack their attachment to what was previously perceived as a needed form, or as you saw it, body, the best shape possible is taken to further one on their journey through Heaven. Meanwhile, as you will shortly experience in the final manifestations of Heaven, while you see in its representative form that the being we follow is primarily in its most essential and true state, there are still trace elements of echo of self-conception remaining which must finally be released before a being may find its way to the farthest reaches one's journey may ultimately take.

"So, when a being has finally excised virtually all the burdensome excess that is still held onto so strongly by that being, the being regroups its essential self, along with those trace remnants too fine to be removed in the seventh manifestation, and the being journeys onward to the eighth manifestation. And here we now find ourselves following this being, just recently on its way to the eighth manifestation of Heaven.

"I would be remiss in my duties if I didn't point out that at this point on the journey through Heaven, even at this stage, even though it has never happened and more likely than not will never happen, even at this point it is just barely possible that a being may cease to continue their journey, and as a result, reincarnate. It hasn't happened, and probably to an infinitesimal degree won't happen, but it can happen."

Thinking, processing the meaning of the driver's explanation of the seventh manifestation, a question occurred to Tim. "You say that those I saw . . . chopping the beings up . . . that those were angels. What was the red bag-looking thing on their heads?"

"Please try to understand, Tim, all of this that you have seen, it is but a vague representation of what this place really is at best. Do you not remember Tola'El? A brief glimpse at one angel should make the need for the obscured appearance of tens of hundreds of angels self-evident. Such a sight would take you many epochs to recover from, if your previous reactions to the other manifestations are any indication.

"You are here only to have a vague appreciation for some semblance of a concept of what one bound for Heaven must pass through to achieve the greatest level of potential possible for a being. The true form of angels is not why you are here, and besides, as incomprehensible as Heaven is for you to grasp, times ten is the true form of a single angel, let alone a thousand or two."

Tim considered the driver's words in silence for what felt like half an hour. As he considered, and contemplated, and tried to reconcile the odd notion that all he had perceived undergoing transition throughout Heaven would become eventually as the odd, glowing, gold ball hovering in front of the bus, he wondered what he might possibly perceive in the eighth manifestation of Heaven. He stared at the ball of gold glow in front of the bus intently and thought about himself in relation to it, while considering the possible truth of his own 'soul.'

He perceived a darkness ahead of the sphere of golden light the bus followed. As the bus passed a final pair of torches, one on either wall of the cave, he perceived a quick darkening of the cave around him and became uneasy. He found darkness once again less than a comfort.

"We're almost to the end of your journey, buddy. No use getting tense about things now. Besides, what could you possibly see at this point that would send you into a shock similar to any you've come to previously?" At these words, Tim was more apprehensive than ever about whatever place they were entering. That which the driver spoke was the very thing that had passed through his mind so many times before, and he found that that very question came usually with a more than adequate answer.

Suddenly the golden glow of the orb hovering before the bus was the only source of light he could perceive, and practically the only thing he could see. The vague outline of the driver turned its head, but even without the driver uttering the words, which he did, he would have known that they had entered the eighth manifestation of Heaven.

Book 11
Manifestation 8: The Essentials

The bus rolled slowly into the darkness, led by the light of the orb of gold it followed. Tim found his gaze drawn to the orb's reflection in the path of water. He felt a touch of awe to feel a deep serenity and quiet appreciation at the sight of the simple, golden disc shimmering in the middle path beneath its source hovering forward. He marveled even more noticing that around the reflecting disc of light cast by the light of the orb, the water rippled. He reflected upon the beauty and the degree to which this simple sight seemed to pull a certain feeling of peace forward within him. He felt himself sink into a deep relaxation and feeling of relief as well as release as he kept his gaze upon the few details able to reach his eyes through the darkness from the water.

He could make out a slight reflection rising off the road of gold, but this light was faint and paled next to the perception of the merger where the illumination of the sphere met with the liquid. The clouds at this point were hardly visible at all. He could make out few details in the bus now, but mostly, the vehicle within which he traveled was only a vague outline to his sight. Tim, without much struggle, resigned himself to the change in setting resulting in his limited sight, and with a strange sense of gratitude that arose seemingly without cause, allowed himself to feel joy at the subtly amazing marriage of light and darkness that took place before him upon the path he traveled.

The bus had rolled slowly behind the orb for some time when he noticed that the sphere the bus followed seemed to be gaining in distance from the bus. He noted without much contemplation that it seemed either the bus was gradually slowing, or the orb was gradually increasing in speed. Having thought this, he again let his thoughts slip away, relinquishing control once again to a quiet reflection and appreciation of the simplicity of his current perceptions.

Watching the hovering sphere with silent repose, he was taken aback to see the sphere, now many feet ahead of the bus, suddenly vanish. Left in total darkness, he became a bit frightened and had something of a longing for the return of the light.

He felt a great uncertainty about how he should feel in this newly perceived darkness when he caught sight of several rays of light piercing the gloom before him without warning. The bus turned a corner and slowed very gradually before coming to a halt. He felt a wave of elation wash over what he had been becoming just moments ago.

Hovering in the darkness all around the bus, he saw that in this place he was surrounded by hundreds of glowing, golden spheres like the one they had followed behind since leaving the seventh manifestation of Heaven. Where once his path was dully illuminated by one sphere, now many spheres cast a great deal of light, illuminating every detail of his surroundings.

About twenty feet or so in front of the bus, he saw that the three paths appeared to end at the very large side of what looked like a very large triangle. The triangle lay flat and even with the road of gold, and was met by identical paths on its other two sides. He saw now three sets of paths of water, roads of gold, and layers of cloud; each tri-pathed set stopping at a side of the triangle, each side of which was of equal length. Each path on each side went out in their respective directions and disappeared into the darkness behind it. The triangle glowed of a soft white light. In the angles between the paths of clouds, he could discern only darkness.

He now saw no cave walls. Aside from the paths, the triangle, the bus, and the orbs of light, all there appeared to be was darkness, blackness. Behind the furthest spheres of light, he thought he could make out the hazy forms of a few beings sitting in what appeared to be postures of deep meditation, like the vague outlines of lotus flowers floating delicately upon a pond of infinity.

All around him, he saw golden globes hovering silently, serenely in the darkness, like glowing bulbs of gilded light hovering in midair without the need for a chain to hold them where they belonged. Each sphere gave off a beautiful radiance which merged with the light of the other spheres, creating in turn an even greater radiance, shedding light on all things present and giving a clarity to the infinite obscurity which stood next to that which the light illuminated. He felt harmony and warmth as he perceived himself touched by the light, and felt a great serenity cleanse him as he saw the spheres of gold hovering peacefully in the apparent infinity.

Some spheres seemed to slowly wander within the space they hovered. Other spheres seemed to stay perfectly still, floating in no direction, and apparently content exactly where they were. Some wandered around the others as though aimlessly. Several roamed within the spaces of apparent nothingness in precise patterns of movement. The spheres stayed at no particular level or height and were spread out in every direction. Some spheres were more or less opaque than the one they had followed, some almost completely clear, discernable perhaps only by a faint gleam of reflection caused by the light of the other spheres, if not its own vague brilliance, but they were all about the same size and all exactly the same shape. Here, amongst these spheres of light, Tim, with full resignation to the softening of his limbs, found himself, completely and totally, relaxed.

"They are beautiful, aren't they?" The driver spoke softly. "Just as in other manifestations, at times a sphere may be seen to spontaneously appear, as a being may find its way straight to the eighth manifestation at the time of death of its body, and then when they appear, they may be of any of the many consistencies of 'transparency' that you perceive.

"As I told you before, this is the eighth manifestation of Heaven. This is where the journeyers of the paths of Heaven come to make the final preparations necessary for entering into the most absolute manifestations of Heaven; what you might call the ninth manifestation.

"You see here beings almost as they truly are, now lacking all but the slightest traces of their former superimposed echoes of self-conception. Here these beings dwell in an almost totally free state, radiating great joy to be closer to that which they truly are than they have known for a very long time. These beings experience here *something*, which you would call very close to happiness to no longer have to endure the types of suffering associated with carrying a form that they were not meant to carry forth after their lives. Here, closer to the truth of themselves than these beings have ever known, they settle, for a time, at peace perceiving the closest experience to freedom they can 'remember' ever having known. This is what you might call the most difficult manifestation to overcome, for this reason.

"While close to their truest and purest state of being, these entities are close to moving on to the final and infinite manifestations of Heaven, but generally the time each one takes to move on varies widely. They feel that they must inevitably complete their journey and find their final dwelling in eternity, but knowing such a level of peace, serenity, and truth so much greater than any they have previously known, the urgency to complete their journey subsides and loses momentum as they find themselves rid of all but the slightest and almost imperceptibly subtle remnants of suffering. There is no regeneration of parts at this point, and that which lies in the next manifestation is not only beyond *your* ability to comprehend, but in their current state, it is also beyond *theirs.* They have something reminiscent of what you might call a 'hunch,' however, about what they might lose by completing their journeys, and it can take them a very long time to part with that last residue of what in ignorance they still consider to be 'themselves.' Having little reason to move on, many beings will spend the length of lifetimes and even up to eons here before they eradicate their final layers of false self and pass into the ninth manifestation of Heaven. Likewise of course, some take anywhere from what you would call years, months, days, minutes, seconds, but then on the other hand, here time is virtually meaningless, since these beings have no reason to be in a rush, or likewise not to be. The nature of this place, being predisposed ultimately to be liable to take any length out of an infinite choice of 'time,' some find their way to the ninth manifestation rather directly and expeditiously, comparatively speaking, whereas others, not so much.

"All that glitters is not gold, Tim. That layer of these beings, which you perceive as gold, in truth is the final impurity that remains in otherwise pure beings. Before a being may enter the final manifestation of Heaven, before they are *naturally* drawn into the final manifestation, they must lose that final false layer separating them from those others who have found their way to their greatest possibility. Here they may experience the great, for lack of better word, light, which they find as the truth of themselves. But there, in their purest and truest state, that light is shared with all others who have come to the end of a very great, and usually long, journey. The loss of separation becomes the gain of *true* freedom, of which here they receive not but the slightest taste. When, with the help of the final light of the Great Gateway of Unity of Tri-Segmentation, which you perceive before you now, a being realizes the final impurities to which they still cling, and as a result realize the whole truth of 'themselves,' they may finally move on and pass into realization of the ninth and final manifestation of Heaven.

"Look there, Tim. Do you see that sphere, there? That sphere floating thirty feet or so away, the one hovering slowly toward us?" The driver pointed toward the front window, a little to the right.

It took Tim a moment or two to pick out of the hundreds of spheres hovering everywhere the one to which the driver pointed, but finally he did see the sphere the driver indicated moving slowly toward the bus. He nodded his head to imply that he did in fact see the sphere.

"Now watch that sphere very closely, my boy," continued the driver, "and you will see a sight that sometimes cannot be seen a second time for what you would perceive as millennia."

Tim watched intently as slowly the sphere drifted toward the bus. It floated quietly and serenely past and around the other spheres in its direct path, and gradually came closer and closer to the bus. Slowly the sphere floated downward under another sphere. Then, slowly the sphere floated around the next. Then again, it took its time as it rose above another sphere. Every foot closer to the bus felt like the passing of many minutes, but the sphere did move quickly enough that he could perceive that it was, in fact, in motion.

After watching the sphere move for what felt like some time, the sphere looked to be about ten feet or so closer to the bus than it had when he had begun watching it. Glancing down briefly, he noticed that the sphere, at its current position, was apparently directly over the center of the triangle of white light. Looking up again, he noticed that the sphere was no longer in motion. The sphere hovered perfectly still, now nine feet or so above the center of the triangle, making no movement whatsoever.

He watched as he saw that the orb, hovering above the glowing triangle of pure radiance, was becoming brighter. As the orb became brighter, he noticed that the orb also grew clearer. A moment or two after he noticed the sphere begin to brighten and lighten, he also saw that, though barely perceptibly, the sphere was beginning to lower straight down toward the center of the triangle. He kept his gaze firmly fixed on the sphere as slowly it simultaneously floated lower and grew brighter and clearer by degrees. The feelings of warmth already surrounding and penetrating Tim grew as he perceived the light grow in the sphere he watched gently descend. Though he perceived that the sphere lowered apparently incredibly slowly, he felt as though he didn't care; as though he found himself watching in a state of virtual timelessness in which he could gladly do nothing but watch the descension of this sphere for the rest of eternity.

About three feet above the triangle the orb, now almost pure light and near perfect transparency, hovered and came to a stop. The light abruptly brightened at a much quicker rate as any and all remnants of an outer shell vanished, and the white light that began to emerge from the sphere completely replaced any gold light that had still emanated from the sphere just moments before. All at once, the sphere suddenly shone forth a radiant, blinding white light and, just as suddenly as the light poured fourth, it immediately subsided, replaced by the dimmer golden conglomeration of light emanating from the other spheres that had been prominent previous to the enlightening of the sphere that Tim had been observing. In the space around the area where the sphere of light had been just a moment ago, a fine dust of gold shined and shimmered in the air, falling lightly and dissolving into the triangle glowing white.

Tim felt a great calm and peace wash over him, and the driver began to speak. "The being you have just perceived dwells now and forevermore in the ninth and final manifestation of Heaven, Tim. After a long journey through many lives and many paths, it comes to the ultimate state of being, fully integrated with the universe by way of its journey to the highest manifestation of this place which *you* can most closely identify by the word 'Heaven.' Blessed be this being to endure all that needed be endured, that it may dwell in infinite light, joined in timelessness with those who came before. Blessed be all creation that another being has come to full realization of what *you* may most closely call truth."

Book 12
Manifestation 9: Cloud None

"You come now close to the end of *your* journey, Tim. Between you and your destination of that realm which *you* would refer to as 'Hell' is your passing through the final manifestation of Heaven. I will let you off at your destination, but you must pass through the final manifestation of Heaven alone."

Despite the great calm pervading Tim during his time in the eighth manifestation, at the driver's words he began to feel a slight touch of unease commence within. At the thought that only one more phase of his journey was left before he would spend what he supposed would be a *very* long time in Hell, he began to become even more uneasy.

"The ninth manifestation is now directly before you, Tim," the driver continued. "You have but to exit the bus, walk down the path you choose, and walk into the Final Great Gateway of Unity of Tri-Segmentation, and you will experience directly the final manifestation. How long you reside there before coming back to the bus and completing your journey is up to you. With eyes closed, and it is important that you understand that I mean this quite literally, for if your eyes are not held tightly shut as you pass into the manifestation you will return to the bus instantly, you may directly experience the truth of the manifestation as one who has made the journey and come to the end. When your eyes open, however, you will *see* the truth of the manifestation, and in that moment of knowing the whole truth, both inside and out, since you are of such composition as you are, you will not be able to hold onto the reality of the greatest possibilities one may come to. Having not prepared yourself properly, you may not stay and will return once again to your journey through the lower realms of your being's existence. With your eyes shut, you will know the truth, but you will not see. With your eyes open, you will see the truth, but you will not be correctly prepared to remember or understand the unity of that which you see and that which you know, and so you will return to your journey, on this bus, in Hell.

"Keep your eyes shut, and you will remain in Heaven for all of eternity if you choose. Open your eyes, and soon thereafter you will find yourself in Hell. Have you heard me fully, Tim?"

Tim considered the driver's words for a moment before slowly, gravely, nodding his head and responding, "Yes. I heard."

"Then, when your eyes are open, I will see you on the other side, Tim." These last words leaving the driver's lips, the front door of the bus drew back on its hinges, and ever so slowly, Tim began to stand.

Down one step, two steps, three steps, Tim descended one-by-one the stairs that in a different time had begun a long journey. With each footfall he now felt an end to that which had begun draw near. The first step brought reflection. The second step brought anticipation. The third step brought a sense of finality, suppressive in its inevitability, and yet oddly acceptable, as though it was somehow obvious despite his inability to name exactly why or how. And then, he was off the bus.

The now familiar feel of the gold-paved road felt cool and smooth beneath his feet. The door of the bus shut quickly behind him, and he turned to look at the bus. He considered the journey he had made upon the bus; the first time he had heard the bus's door snap shut. Just as the beginning of his journey, the door sounded now too with a certain sort of abrupt decisiveness beyond dispute. He glanced briefly at the paths he would not take to the left, having no desire to try again to walk on water, and decided that neither would he like to end his journey with his perspective in the clouds, no matter how cool and almost inviting in another time this path may have been.

Tim looked to the few remaining steps of the road that lay before him and began to urge his legs in the direction he knew to be inevitable, forward. The flat, glowing triangle of pure white radiance seemed much bigger to him now that he was out of the bus and on his own two feet, and seemed to grow exponentially in size with each slow, subsequent footfall.

He felt himself get warmer with each step he took, but not as he had on previous occasions when moving forward meant being engulfed by an oppressive, blazing kind of heat. He felt now a simple warmth growing that did nothing but soothe his nerves, albeit very little, as he grew closer to the inevitable. Now he found himself between the bus and the triangle, ten feet from an unknown inevitability in one direction, and ten feet from a not always pleasant and fully known certainty in the other. Only ten feet away, the great triangle of light was very large before him.

Eight steps later, the triangle glowed bright at his toes and radiated a warmth that seemed almost to engulf him as though through mere proximity he himself was slowly being turned to a pure, white light. He held his right foot above the triangle and felt his form lighten as though it were in fact light, and looking down, he could not distinguish his foot from the warm, bright glow which it was held over. He brought his right leg back next to his left leg again, and he felt the sure, though annoyingly heavy, feeling of his foot return. Looking down, he was again quite certain of his foot's presence.

He gazed for some time at his fate, basking in the warm glow of this odd, final gateway. He looked again at the bus. He saw the front side of the bus and the driver looking directly, intently, and serenely at him from behind the bus's front window, from behind the steering wheel of the bus; his dead father's face looking at him with serenity to see the completion of his passenger's fate. He looked to the clouds to his right and ran his hand through the cool, crisp moistness of a path made for a vehicle he supposedly at present could not conceive. He looked at the water to his left and ran his fingers through the path, cool and wet, apparently untouched by the beings that floated over the path to the completion of *their* long journeys. He considered again the smooth coolness of the golden road he himself had traveled upon, and considered that in a moment he would know the end brought by each of the varied ways running parallel to one another.

He looked again to the bright, white glow of the triangle he faced. He considered where he had been, where he now stood, and where he must go. He considered the great warmth in front of him, somehow soothing him through his fright, beckoning him forward. He tightly closed his eyes, took a very large, very deep breath through his nose from his belly, released through his nose, breathed in again the same way, and jumped forward.

Tim felt himself rise upward for two brief moments, felt his self pause briefly in midair, and then felt himself begin to descend. Another two moments later, he felt his feet dissolve into pure warmth, followed quickly by the rest of his body. He felt his chin, nose, and finally his head disappear into unity with something much greater than his body had been.

He felt as though he had become pure light and was joined with something far greater than the previous individuality he had experienced as he joined together with all other light that composed the universe of which he was now a part; but he saw nothing. Blackness. Darkness. Not even blackness, not even darkness, for those words represent more than that which he saw. Absolute lack of anything was all. There was nothing. No-thing. Not even "Tim" existed here, or rather, nowhere. Absolute void, absence, nothing. No-thing. There simply wasn't as was. It wasn't is, it wasn't isn't, and not even that. There simply was-not. Not being. No-thing. And then, from nothing to see, his eyes were opened.

Though, somewhere, somehow he knew he had eyes, and that they were open as he saw light, the light was so complete that it was as though his perception of his own eyes dissolved into light. All his senses, touch, taste, audio, olfactory, all perceived light; all were light. Warmth flooded him, *was* him, he was it, it was everything. There was no motion, no beginning, no end, just light, just what was.

Like waves of joy, Tim felt connected to everything where he was NOW. He felt all of Heaven, perceived the unity of every manifestation his eyes had before witnessed. He felt all of Earth, the unity of the Earth with its universe. He felt as though all of the universe connected and harmonized for the sake of what he felt the perfect unity he experienced to be. Flashes of vague recollections of concepts such as war and music and flowers and water and mountains and murder and feet and galaxies and atoms and algae and ants and humans and labor and destruction and lint and how it all interwove, interconnected to be the vast tapestry of the perfect infinity that all connected to here, now, him, everything, everywhere. All was joined in perfection complete unto itself. Time joined itself in all places and became meaningless. Space and difference did not exist. He was one with light, with warmth, with existence, with everything. Joy flooded and danced in his consciousness; the universe sang with ecstasy a tune without melody or sound, and yet which resonated through all he knew and perceived.

Brighter and brighter he felt himself become as more connected with everything he felt, and less and less an identity of his own did he realize. The word "Tim" became meaningless, as he was so much more; becoming everything, realizing everything by being everything, by being. He was that which he was in perfect harmony and in perfect accordance as he must be. He had realized why he was what he was, so that now he could be as he was, as everything, EVERY-thing. The universe flooding through him as he flooded through the universe, and through all, as all, this was, is, will be, all, universe. And he was.

And only good, and only joy, and only what was as it must be for the sake of what it is. Reason for reason's sake. Cause as the effect to be the cause. Realization of perfection and joy and rapture and happiness and ecstasy, just to be. And he knew what was as it must be, and if one word could encompass, only good could be that word. Tim, in this state, in this, what the driver called the ninth manifestation of Heaven, knew Love. Only Love. In Love. All Love. Everything Love. Just Love. Love.

And without thought, as continuing to spread into the infinite perfection, knowing the perfect love that was the infinite truth of all that existed, with all his being, from the deepest recesses of whatever was left of the being called "Tim" came a great expression and sound of booming laughter, the great joy that his last vestiges of individuality could create to harmonize that "Tim" with everything. And the universe rang from infinite end to infinite end with pure laughter from the very heart and soul of that which knew perfection, truth, light. Now, laughter had become that which was throughout all and everything, as though in perfect unity and harmony there was only one big laugh and nothing more, and nothing less.

But despite the nothing seen giving way to the unity felt, Tim wasn't Heaven-bound, he was Hell-bound. He did not know until after his eyes were open the whole being that he was, and he *could* see, but his own existence did not negate his own existence, and *Tim* did exist. Without enduring the tempering of each manifestation of Heaven, but merely passing through, he could not stay here in nowhere, in the final realization of Heaven. Though close to unity, without proper temperance, he existed, and with eyes open he had no choice but to separate from no-thing into some-thing, and so he began to become again that which he was, separate once more from that which simply is. And he began to remember himself. He began to remember his form. He began to remember his own existence, though perhaps still a part of all, only a part. He felt his body return. He raised a hand before his face and saw it clearly next to no thing. Some thing. Some-thing. He felt a thought knowing his hand, and body, and eyes, and sight, and compared nothing to something. No-thing to some-thing. And he felt feelings, distinguishing between the Love in unity and a new feeling, Fear, in continuing separation. And he began to *feel* separate, and he began to feel afraid. And he then remembered his own, unique, individual voice as at the top of *his* lungs he began to scream. Then, he felt as though through infinite nothing, he himself, as something, fell.

And Tim felt himself fall. And he fell. And fell. And fell. And fell. And fell.

Tim fell into a bus.

Book 13
The Choice of Where to Hang One's Hat or Things You *Could* Make Out of Forests and Trees

Love and fear on Tim's confused lips, he looked out the right-side window, the window closest to where he sat, and watched his neighborhood pass before his eyes. Familiar cars, and trees, and houses, and dogs, and cats, and people, and lawns, and numbers all sped by the window out from which he gazed. And he saw his own house draw near. As the bus slowed, the words of the driver penetrated his ears. "Welcome, Tim, to Hell."

"Hell? But this looks like Earth," gasped Tim in disbelief.

"My God," chuckled the driver through a grin in a low voice while shaking his head from side to side. "You kids can never seem to see the Purgatory for the Hell." And the bus stopped in front of Tim's house.

And the door of the bus swung open. And Tim stood and felt the floor of the bus under his feet, felt each step of the bus under his feet, felt the concrete of the sidewalk under his feet. He felt a cool breeze wash over his face after the warm sun. He heard the songs of a chirping bird drift down from the tree in his front lawn. He saw a snail creeping along slowly down the sidewalk to his house, a path of slime trailing behind it. He stepped up and felt the cool graininess of the concrete of his patio beneath his feet. He heard the door of the bus close and the rumble of the bus moving forward. He gazed over his shoulder to watch it roll down the street and pass out of sight. He felt for and removed a key from his pocket and inserted the key into the door's lock. He turned the key and heard the lock unlock with a definitive "click."

Tim opened the door and walked into his house.